DON [

COAS

TUNA

A Mallard Cove Adventure Novel

Coastal Adventure Series
Volume 4

FLORIDA REFUGEE PRESS, LLC
2020

Library of Congress PCN Data
Rich, Don
Coastal Tuna/Don Rich
(A Mallard Cove Adventure Novel)
Florida Refugee Press LLC

Edit/Proofreading by: Tim Slauter
Cover Photo by: iStock Photo

Published by FLORIDA REFUGEE PRESS, LLC, 2020
Crozet, VA
Copyright © 2020 by Don Rich

Dedication

To all of those brave people who are on the front lines every day. From the soldier or sailor standing watch in a foreign land or the deck of a ship, to the police and firefighters, and the doctors and nurses. Whether the enemy they guard against is human, or a microscopic virus. Thanks to all of you for making our lives that much better, so that we may continue to live in health, and in Freedom.

April 9, 2020
Crozet, VA

Preface

Galax, Massachusetts is the kind of place where you would expect to find rough-looking commercial boats and the tough crews who run them. And you wouldn't be disappointed. Most of these men and women are just scraping by, making a living on the water not just because it's the only thing they know how to do, but because they love it. They know that they'll never get rich by fishing, at least not in monetary terms. But if you offered them jobs making two or even three times what they do now and it meant moving inland away from the water, almost all would turn it down in a heartbeat. Ten years ago a different opportunity did come along for a handful of them right here in Galax, changing their lives as well as the town forever. Ironically, it had come from the son of a fishing family, someone who had decided he wanted a different future for himself. He was determined to get as far away from Galax as possible and make money, *real* money. There was no way that commercial fishing was going to be his destiny.

For as long as he could remember, Lorne Gillam had been fascinated by television. Not by the physical thing that sits in your living room, but by the behind the scenes production of the shows that it brings into all of our lives. He knew there was a ton of money there for the right person, a clever person with good ideas and the drive to see them through. He was the son of a fishing captain, and one of the few who had left Galax to chase his dreams.

Lorne became deeply involved in this industry that was about as far from fishing as it could be. Though one day he returned to the small town where he had grown up. bringing with him an idea that would end up putting this seaside town on the map. It was something not all of the locals were happy about.

Reality television was quickly becoming the hottest thing on cable. Most of it was staged garbage, and as far from actual reality as it could be. Somehow Lorne had managed to convince a few investors that America was ready to see inside the lives of some real people: the tuna fishermen and women of Galax, Massachusetts. Little did he know how right he was. The show was called *Tuna Hunters*, and by the end of the first season, it became one of cable's hottest new shows. As its creator and executive producer, Lorne had now become a hot property within the industry. He did so by using people that he had little respect for, people he had grown up with, the hard-working people of the commercial fishing fleet.

When Lorne left, he had wanted nothing further to do with any of the fishermen. Now, a decade later, he was the richest man in Galax because of them. The fishing boat crews he originally hired for the series had all been paid between twenty and thirty thousand dollars per boat that first year. To them, it was "found" money, and in some cases, it was even more than their cut from the sale of their tuna catch that season. Now several had become waterfront celebrities, not just here in Massachusetts, but up and down the US coastlines and even inland.

These days a few of the more flamboyant and popular cast members were pocketing well over a million dollars per year in pay from the show, as well as personal appearance fees at boat shows and seafood festivals. With this rise in income, their boats had become newer, longer, and faster. But fame had also come at a huge cost for some, their unexpected windfall fueling growing egos as well as substance abuse binges ranging from alcohol to opioids. This influx in money also took its toll on the fabric of the town; straining relationships, breaking marriages, and in one, an overdose case had become a fatality.

There had been four fatalities when you added in the loss of a Galax boat off the Carolina coast. The father/son crew had become driven by the desire to win that season no matter how rough the seas. They were also driven by Lorne, who demanded more and more fish at the weigh-ins. Empty boats were no good for ratings, but scenes of waves breaking over bows and crews struggling to land huge fish in big seas were television gold. Man pitted against nature was a theme that people loved, and advertisers were willing to pay big money to be a part of.

Every member of the cast and crew knew that by being pushed to work in such weather it wasn't a question of if someone would lose a boat, but when. That wasn't something that concerned Lorne. He had worked too hard to build the *Tuna Hunter* franchise, and if this bunch of pantywaists didn't want to work as hard as him, there were a ton of others that would jump at a chance to be on his show. This was the attitude that would ultimately cost a crew and a cameraman their lives.

A decade ago Lorne had started with an artistic vision of the show he wanted to create. Things seemed so much simpler then, but the pressures had increased in proportion to the profits. These days he had become less of an artist and more of a businessman. His responsibilities included having to negotiate salaries with the lawyers of the people who were now the stars of the show, the very people he had made rich. Cast holdouts over salaries, egos, and jealousy were all part of what he now dealt with daily. At least he didn't have to go out on the boats himself anymore, he had "people" for that. His producer-cinematographers rode along on each boat, with duties similar to those of local news station crews. They're there to record what happens, and during the slow periods, they also encourage a little improvised drama to keep things interesting.

Lorne's newest headache though involved the town politics down in the Carolinas where they filmed the latest and most popular incarnation of the show, "*Tuna Hunters – Rebels Versus Yanks*". Several new council people had been elected down there, and they were claiming the town was being severely undercompensated for its use as the show's backdrop. Two council members had been voted off this year after they were accused of taking personal bribes from the show. It wasn't true, but you know how rumors can run wild in every political season, especially in a small town. Their replacements were now trying to flex their newfound political muscles by squeezing the show. They were demanding quadruple the amount of fees in return for Lorne's production company's permits to film there this coming winter. Apparently, the exponential increase in tourism, charter boat and hotel bookings, as well as meals served by the local restaurants that also catered the meals of the production staff wasn't enough for them. All this of course brought in a relatively huge amount of tax revenue, not to mention the increase in property values they had enjoyed. These political newbies had a classic case of short-sightedness and greed.

So, this morning Lorne was thinking over this latest debacle, finishing breakfast in the nook off of his kitchen and staring out the window. The nook's huge bay window offered a stunning southern view of the waterfront. His home was on a rocky peninsula that jutted far out into the harbor, almost thirty feet above the water. But this morning his thoughts kept him preoccupied and unable to see and enjoy the view from his massive brick home. Gull's Nest was almost two-hundred and fifty years old and was the most expensive residential property in Galax. Since the day that it had been built it had been the ultimate local symbol of power, having been constructed by the most wildly successful captain in the town at the time. Like Lorne, his real success had been in business, not by working on a boat himself, but by buying up boats from owners that were in financial straits. Through his efforts, the captain had cobbled together one of the largest fishing fleets in New England. Because of this he was both revered, envied, as well as despised, much like Lorne today.

Gull's Nest stood atop the last point of land the Galax fishing fleet passed as they left the harbor and headed out to sea. It was a constant reminder to the crews that ventured out of how safe the home's owner was back on land, while they worked for him risking their lives in the cold, deep, and often angry New England waters. This was something that hadn't changed in over in two centuries.

Lorne left his dishes on the table for his cook to clear and wash, then checked his watch and grabbed his briefcase. He wasn't in a hurry; his chartered NetJet wasn't due to depart for another half hour. Not that it mattered, even if he was late it would wait for him; he was the only passenger this morning on the flight down to Carolina. He had another meeting scheduled with the town council down there, hopefully, the last one. Lorne had dropped a bombshell on them last week: accept his terms, or this winter he would move the show to another town. They knew that for them this would mean going back to being a ghost town in those off-season months. Many folks over the past couple of years had become used to the extra money which came from their year-round employment. Losing it would now mean having to get used to being laid off in the winters again. That was something they would be sure to remember on election day.

Lorne had expected a call from the new mayor accepting his terms, but instead he received an email asking him to meet again today with the town council. He had agreed, but instead of going down to negotiate, he was going to add a deadline to his recent ultimatum, upping the pressure. He wanted to look into their eyes as he told them, letting each of them see that he was dead serious. He wasn't about to be held up by some backwater politicians that were stupid enough to think that they had any leverage over him at all. Oh, and about that deadline? Ten minutes from that very moment.

Lorne walked out through the front door and headed to his brand new bright red Range Rover. It was a mobile symbol of his success, and he loved it. Over five-hundred and fifty horsepower, with black and silver carbon fiber trim and quilt-stitched brown leather interior. It had cost him just under two-hundred grand, but it was the only one of this model this side of Boston. It left no doubt about who was driving it as he came roaring down the street, and it screamed that Lorne had indeed reached the absolute pinnacle of success. The masculine smell and feel of the interior as well as the growl of the supercharged engine gave him a thrill that no other car he'd ever owned had even begun to approach. He hated leaving it out in the salt air overnight, but the old detached carriage house/garage on the estate was being renovated, and it would be at least another month before it was finished. Besides, he did like the way it looked, sitting out in front of the house on his cobblestone driveway.

He opened the car door, and the hidden running boards instantly extended, opening the circuit on a hidden microswitch. Climbing into the driver's seat and closing the door behind him, the running boards quickly retracted, again coming into contact with the microswitch. This switch hadn't been installed at the Rover factory, and neither had the circuitry to which it was attached. It was the trigger for a device that now detonated with such force that it pulverized Lorne's body; he was never even the slightest bit aware of what happened. The pressure also blew out or broke all the glass windows in the front of Gull's Nest, as well as

9

several of the workers' pickup trucks in front of the carriage house, eighty feet from the blast.

The sound of the explosion carried across the open water, echoing off the harbor front buildings more than a half-mile away. Many along the waterfront instantly wondered and speculated as to the cause, but one of them knew, prompting a small grim smile that no one else noticed. The deaths and the personal destruction would stop now, as people started coming back to their senses. Greed would no longer override safety, and crews could now pick and choose their trips without having to ignore the weather. The pressure and recklessness would be history. Without Lorne, *Tuna Hunters* should now be just as dead as he was.

Chapter 1
Magothy, Virginia

I love going to boatyards. In fact, I can't ever recall a time when I didn't, except maybe when something on one of my boats was broken, or when I had to pay the bill for the repairs. Still, that isn't the boatyard's fault, and I'm darn glad that such a place exists where I can have my boats routinely maintained, and occasionally repaired. Oh, and built. I almost forgot that part, probably because it's still new to me. It's also why I'm at this particular boatyard today.

But I'm getting ahead of things. Let me introduce myself, my name is Marlin Denton. I'm also known as "Shaker", and occasionally even "Shake and Bake" but those are marina nicknames, given to me by an old friend, Captain Bill "Baloney" Cooper. I'll get around to Bill later. Anyway, I'm thirty-two years old, about average height with shaggy sandy hair. And while I'm not what you would exactly describe as skinny, I'm no longer chubby or fat, either. I'm also engaged to the best woman in the world, Kari Albury. Together we are building a houseboat, or rather, a house*barge*, which again is the reason I'm here at the boatyard today. This is Kari's cousin Carlton's boatyard, one of the best on the Eastern Shore of Virginia, or as those of us that live here call it, ESVA. I'm just checking on our progress since *Tied Knot* is scheduled to be christened and launched in the morning. That's the name of our new floating home, a play on the name of my vintage wooden 42' Chris Craft, *Why Knot*, which we currently live aboard.

As I round the corner of the building and see *Tied Knot* now sitting outside of the shed where she was built, I'm taken aback at how big she looks out in the sunshine. The building crew had just pulled her out into the "railyard" where her steel-wheeled construction cradle will eventually be transferred onto the "ways" for tomorrow's launching. At seventy-eight feet long by twenty-four feet wide and three decks high, she looks kind of like a miniature cruise ship that's minus a pointed bow and rounded stern. I climbed up a ladder that was leaning against the hull and stepped off onto the covered aft entrance deck, passing through the main entrance door into the salon. That's where I found Carlton, going over a final 'punch list' with his crew's foreman. He looked up as I entered and smiled at me.

"Quite a different sight now that she's out of the shed eh, Marlin?"

I nodded, "She looks twice as big, Carlton. Are we still on schedule for tomorrow morning?"

"You bet. I was just going over some last little details with Jack here that he will make sure are covered today. With no engines to align, no raw water systems to check, and no sea trial needed, you'll be set to go as soon as she floats off the cradle."

I nodded again, "I hired the Williams brothers and their two deadrise boats to pull her down to Mallard Cove."

Like I said, *Tied Knot* is a *housebarge*. Meaning that she has no propulsion system of her own; she's dependent on other vessels to pull or push her when she needs to move. But her compartmentalized shovel-nosed barge hull should need little to no maintenance, and her slip is just seven miles away from here if she does. Hopefully, the only reason that she'll ever need to be hauled out again on the ways would be if a big mid-Atlantic hurricane were to head our way. Fortunately, those don't hit around here as often they do in the tropics.

Carlton and his foreman Jack led me on what would probably be the final tour before the launching. Kari and I had thought of just about everything we could on *Tied Knot* to make her as comfortable as any land-based home.

12

The lower deck features a master stateroom, a large salon (that's the nautical name for a living room), laundry, galley, bar and dining area. The second deck contains two more staterooms and a central sitting room. The upper deck is all open except for a covered outdoor kitchen complete with a grill and bar amidships. There was also a small enclosed anteroom with circular stairs and an open elevator platform that connects all three decks. Aft there is a seating area with cable railings that will overlook the dock, and up forward is a built-in hot tub and sundeck with a solid knee wall railing for privacy. *Tied Knot* was set up for living and entertaining, and this deck will easily hold three dozen people or more during a party. I can't wait to get her over and into her slip at Mallard Cove Marina.

Mallard Cove is where both Kari's and my offices are located. I'm executive director of the Mid-Atlantic Fisheries Foundation (MAFF), and Kari runs M & S Marina Partners. That's the marina management, acquisition, and design arm of McAlister and Shaw, an ESVA based real estate company owned by our friends Dawn McAlister and Casey Shaw. At only twenty-five years old, you might think that Kari is really young to have the responsibility of a multi-million dollar real estate portfolio, and you'd be right. But spend five minutes with her and you would realize why they not only trust her with it, but also made her a junior partner so that she'd stick with them permanently. She not only oversees the management of this marina complex but is also one of its equity partners.

And before you get the idea that my director gig is all about begging for money in a coat and tie on the cocktail circuit, let me explain. I only own one suit, and it's reserved for weddings and funerals. MAFF is a very low-key and independent organization dedicated to protecting Atlantic fisheries, and it doesn't seek out nor accept outside donations. Because of an interesting transaction that is part of a story from another day, it

13

has an endowment of a little more than three billion dollars. Yes, billion with a "B". Yet our offices don't even have our name on the door. Instead, it says, "Pelican Fleet Management", a company which shares the office space with MAFF. Pelican is made up from my growing group of charter boats and crews that are based at Mallard Cove. We offer parasailing, eco-tours, stand up paddleboarding and private fishing charters. I know, the "private" part sounds snobbish, but it's not. These are the trips that I run myself, with a small list of customers that I know well.

I used to have open charters; meaning that I took anyone who showed up on the dock with cash in hand. But through the years I developed that great list of clients who I am now friends with, and that I love to take out fishing. But I still had to make a living back then, and this meant filling in the rest of the days on my calendar with any other folks who wanted to go. Most of them were great, but occasionally there were those that I wouldn't have minded dumping overboard. Now, thanks to a cash settlement that Kari and I reached with a relative of mine, another of those stories from another day, I can afford to be very choosy about my clients.

I fish out of my two outboards; the first is an eighteen-foot Maverick named *Bone Shaker*. You might already have figured out that "Baloney", the same guy who gave me my nickname, had a hand in picking out this name, too. And I also have an older twenty-six foot Gold Line with twin two hundred horsepower outboards named *Marlinspike*. Fortunately, I named her myself before I met Baloney. So, which boat I use depends on the weather, the target species, and the area where I'm going to fish. I only run offshore in *Marlinspike* on calm days, and also at the mouth of the Chesapeake during the rough fall rockfish season. I use *Bone Shaker* on calm Chesapeake days, and in more "skinny water" on the east side, mostly for blues, mackerel, flounder, reds,

14

and tarpon. Yes, tarpon. It's a little known secret that the farthest north you can catch a tarpon in the USA is around Oyster, Virginia, just a few miles from here. Oh, and with my long time clients, I prefer to use fly rods whenever possible. My charters have provided much of the material for my numerous photos and articles that have appeared in national fishing magazines. I write most of these in the winter, when a lot of the water in the Chesapeake tends to become solid, and I have more time on my hands.

Carlton and I left Jack and his crew to work on the final few items on the punchlist and then climbed back down to the railyard.

"So, Marlin, have you been over and checked out Baloney's new project yet?"

"No. In fact, I haven't seen Baloney in a couple of days. I haven't heard anything about a new project, I just figured he was out on charters."

"Uh, no. He's been all but living here lately. Bobby has been running the boat while he was busy with this. We're just about to raise it now."

"Raise it? What is it, another boat? And you meant haul it, right?" I knew that Bill had been looking at a lot of boats, wanting to buy one and let his mate, Bobby Smith, aka "B2" as in, Baloney 2, run it. B2 had gotten his captain's license half a year ago, but as a young mate, he couldn't yet afford to buy his own boat. Bill saw it as an opportunity for both he and Bobby to make more money and expand the charter business out of Mallard Cove. I figured he must have finally found a rig for Bobby.

"Nope, I meant 'raise it.' You'll see. Let's head over to the slab."

The slab was what everyone called a huge concrete yard with a travelift. That's like a big mobile gantry crane on wheels with several huge nylon straps that are used for hauling and launching boats. Two

15

long, narrow cement piers stick out into the water from the seawall at the slab, designed to allow the travelift to straddle the water between them. The wide, heavy-duty straps are lowered into the water, letting a boat float in place over them. Then they are raised, hauling it out before the gantry moves it to a spot in the yard. Then the boat's keelson is lowered gently onto huge wooden blocks or ties and braced along inside the chines to keep it from tipping over. A boat that's hauled out is referred to as being "up on the hard."

As Carlton and I walked over toward the travelift slip I saw a cabin and a tuna tower protruding from the surface, as well as a bunch of salvage lift bags. But no hull was visible above the murky brown water, and that's when the phrase Carlton had used hit me like a sledgehammer.

I looked at Carlton, "Tell me he didn't."

"I could do that, but I'd be lying." Carlton chuckled after he said it.

As we neared the slab, I spotted Baloney standing at the seawall between the travelift piers. He was easy to miss since he only stood about five feet, five inches tall, with short graying hair and slightly wide shoulders. He was in his early fifties but seldom acted his age, and that can be taken however you want. To put it bluntly, he's a piece of work. And today I could see that he was looking as proud as an expectant father. I began to wonder what the legal process was to have a friend committed.

As we continued toward him, he spotted us approaching, "Oh, hey guys! Big day today!"

I shook my head, "Just tell me you didn't."

"Nah, I didn't sink her."

Well, that part was good. Then I said, "I meant tell me you didn't buy her."

"I'd be lying if I did that, Shaker. Ain't she a beaut!"

Two people using that same phrase within five minutes of each other is not a good sign. And about the "beaut" part; Bill is originally from New Jersey, something about which there is no doubt when you hear him speak.

"Yeah, if you like submarines."

"Hey! That's my new rig you're talking about there, Shake and Bake!"

Bill only uses my longer nickname when he's irritated with me. And he calls me Marlin when he's furious. At least we weren't to that point. Yet.

"O...kay. So, what are you going to do, strip and scrap it?" I was walking on eggshells here. It looked as if he seriously liked this wreck.

"Hell no! I'm gonna fix her up then me and Betty are gonna live aboard her. I'll give the *Dolphin* to Bobby to run, an' this new one's mine!" Another sign that he was irritated with me was that his ever-present and unlit cigar was now rapidly moving back and forth from one corner of his mouth to the other, seemingly by itself. Bill only lights up when he clears the breakwater out on a charter on the *Golden Dolphin*. She's his old smoke-belching forty-eight foot wooden sportfish that was built a lifetime ago up in New Jersey. Not smoking his cheap stogies on land is his wife's strictest rule, since she can't stand the smell. And speaking of Betty, she's a great lady who should be given a medal for having put up with Bill for decades.

"You've got your work cut out for you. Why did it sink anyway?"

Baloney shrugged. "Dunno. We'll figure that out when we get her up on the hard."

He'd had to raise his voice a bit since the gunwales were now above the surface and some of the yard crew had cranked up a pair of gas-powered pumps to start de-watering the hull. Now I could see that this was a flybridge sportfisherman, well over fifty feet long. Then I spotted something that shouldn't have been

17

where it was. No, make that two somethings that were out of place.

"Bill, please tell me those aren't outboards." Two engines on brackets were bolted to the stern.

"Yeah, Shaker, they are. But they're only temporary. In fact, I gotta give 'em back as part of the deal. They were just trying to use them to push her down to Florida for a refit. They hung 'em on the back after she sunk the first time 'cause the diesels are toast."

"Wait, it sunk *twice*?"

"More like wrecked and sunk the first time. See, she was up a river in Jersey behind her owner's house when that freak hurricane hit two years ago. Tossed her up on a pair of pilings that went through the bow and the starboard midships below the waterline."

Now it was starting to make sense, at least as much as it could. Bill loves everything that comes from New Jersey, which he pronounces *Joisey*.

"Anyway, the owner had to dick around with the insurance company for over a year until they replaced her with a new Viking and pulled this one out from behind his house."

The light bulb over my head lit up as I recognized the boat's lines. "So, she's a Viking!"

"Now you're catchin' on, Shaker. A fifty-four convertible, and just over ten years old. Cost way over a million bucks when she was new, and I got her for less than a pair of used motors. The latest owners and the salvage crew were all out of cash, fighting like cats and dogs, and about to end up in court where they'd have all lost more than they already had. They were all blaming each other for it sinking again. Then Carlton had the US Marshalls seize it to make sure he was gonna get paid, 'cause his bill for the salvage and storage was going up real fast, and he hadn't seen any money yet. I jumped in and saved the day by buying her as is, where is."

"But you still have to put in new diesels, new outriggers, new electronics, new wiring and a new interior. You could be darn close to what she cost new when you get through with all that."

Baloney smiled, "I might be if I took her back to the way she was, but I'm makin' her a real charter boat, one that works for a living, not a yacht. No more teak in the cockpit, she's gonna be all fiberglass. Nice enough interior, but paint over fiberglass, not all polished wood and varnish. And see that burned up Hatteras over there?" He pointed to a burned-out hull sitting on the slab. "The insurance company just totaled her. I bought her yesterday, too. The engine room wasn't hurt too bad and never went underwater so the motors are still good and they don't have a lotta hours on 'em. All the AC units, fish box icemaker system, generator, they're all good. A lotta what I need to get this one goin' again. I'm gonna make one rig outta two, and I'll have the fanciest looking and fastest charter boat over at Mallard Cove."

I was starting to do the math in my head. Bill might be onto something with this, depending on how bad the hull damage was. He might just end up with a rig that would charter for a premium. Vikings are thought of as one of, if not *the* best fiberglass production sportfishing boats going. They are fast, decently stable, and their interiors are comparable to what you might find in the most plush private jets. And when you are fishing on a day charter, you only really use the "head" and the salon part of the cabin anyway. The majority of the time you're in the fishing cockpit, and this one will still look like a new Viking once it gets cleaned up. It appeared that the flying bridge hadn't ever been submerged, either.

"You know, Bill, you might not be as crazy as everybody says."

"Thanks, Shak...what?" His head snapped toward me as Carlton and I laughed out loud. "Thanks a lot, you two. Just for that, make sure you bring some good

19

beer this afternoon, I'm in the mood to celebrate, and I haven't been to a meeting in four days."

The meeting he was referring to is what we call our Beer Thirty Bunch. Most of the charter crews and the dock regulars get together around four-thirty in the afternoon to compare notes on the fishing as well as tell a story or two. It's a BYOB kind of thing, except for Bill; he mostly mooches off everyone else. Nobody minds, it's kind of accepted, especially since he is usually the first to share locations with the rest of us when he gets into the fish. We're all working hard to build the reputation of the Mallard Cove charter fleet, of which Bill is the unofficial leader. He is a hoot, so we just look at it like paying the court jester, and it's always worth the price of admission. To tell the truth, I'm looking forward to seeing everyone's faces when Bill tells this story.

Chapter 2

The big pumps made quick work of much of the water inside of Bill's new boat, though some was still coming in. Once most of the extra weight was gone the yard crew was able to haul her out with the travelift which of course stopped the flooding. As the flow reversed it was really easy to see where the water had come from; the crew taking her to Florida had patched the holes in the bottom with plywood that was screwed to the hull and only sealed with silicone. It was a wonder that they had gotten as far as they had. The plywood delaminated underwater, and the patches started to flex and fail. By the time the crew discovered the leak, it was way too late. They had tried to make it to Carlton's travelift slip to save her but fell short. Luckily they had made it up the channel which led a hundred yards back through the marsh flats. They reached the shallow side of the turning basin before she went down. If they had sunk in that channel it would have blocked access to Carlton's business until she could have been raised and moved.

But now despite the gaping holes in the bottom, properly repairing the hull seemed to be far from Baloney's focus. "I'm thinking of goin' with a kinda light green hull color, what do you two think?" Staring up at the hull, Bill had a faraway look on his face, like he was taking in more than just the boat in front of him.

Carlton nodded. "She's got the lines for it, Bill."

"I think you've got a long way to go before you need to start worrying about paint colors, Baloney." Apparently, I wasn't seeing exactly what he and Carlton were, at least not yet.

Baloney frowned at me, "You're getting things backwards, Shaker. You need to look at her as she's gonna be, and work toward that. One of those famous dead sculptor guys said that there's a statue inside

21

every hunk of rock, you just gotta chisel everything else away. *My Mahi* is like that statue, we just have to smooth a few things out, first. And I think she'd look great in light green sitting there next to the *Golden Dolphin*'s yellow hull and *Kembe II*'s orange one. I'm thinking about us tryin' to attract attention like they do down at the Outer Banks."

The Oregon Inlet fleet in North Carolina was famous for its assorted and bright hull colors. I had to admit, Baloney might just have something here. Especially since my thirty-five-foot parasail charter rig, *High Flier*, had a bright red hull and her slip was directly across from the *Dolphin*'s yellow bow. You can't get customers unless you catch their attention, and color was a good way to start.

"*My Mahi*, huh? Nice." I recognized the play off the *Golden Dolphin* name, which was not about the mammal but the fish, whose Hawaiian name is mahi. A few decades ago their more commonly used name was dolphin, or dolphinfish. Then folks became confused back in the early nineteen-sixties when "Flipper" the TV show came out, centered around a bottle-nosed dolphin. American restaurant patrons were horrified, thinking this smart mammal was what they had been eating. So, the fish became re-branded with the more exotic and expensive-sounding Hawaiian name.

Bill grinned. "So, you like what I did there, eh? Mahi? Dolphin?"

"Yeah, yeah, I get it Baloney. You're starting the dolphin fleet."

"Hey! I like the sound of that, Shaker! Yeah, the dolphin fleet! That'll look great on a tee shirt."

Call me crazy, but suddenly I was starting to catch some of Bill's enthusiasm for his new project. Though I was glad that he was doing all the work, not me. At least, that's what I thought at first, but I saw him get this strange look on his face, and I knew right then that I should have left five minutes ago.

"Hey, Shaker, keep this quiet, will ya? I wanna spring it on the gang myself this afternoon. Heck, I'll even buy the beer. You wanna tape up a note on the Captain's Lounge door for me?"

"Ohhh, no. You're not getting me mixed up in this, Baloney! If you are buying the beer, there's a lot more to this."

"You're too suspicious. All I'm asking you to do is tape up a simple note for me; it ain't that hard, and you owe me."

That part took me by surprise, though at this point nothing should have. "How do you figure that I owe you anything? You know, if I was keeping score, you'd probably owe me more than ten cases of beer after you count up all the ones I've given you."

Baloney feigned an indignant and hurt look. "If it weren't for me, you'd still be living aboard *Why Knot* all by your lonesome 'cause you'd have never met Kari."

I knew better. I was just barely beyond the reach of that black hole known as "Baloney Logic" which no doubt would suck me in if I opened my mouth at this point. But I also knew that I had to hear this explanation, no matter the cost.

"Okay, Baloney, I'll bite. How do I owe you for Kari and me getting together when it was 'Linds' who fixed us up?" Lindsay Davis and her other half, Michael "Murph" Murphy, were the main partners in Mallard Cove, as well as Kari and my good friends. They also lived aboard in the marina on another housebarge called *On Coastal Time* which was the original inspiration for *Tied Knot*. They ran private charters on their sixty-foot Merritt sportfisherman, *Irish Luck*.

"If I hadn't told you about the *Cove*, you'd have ended up down at Rudee Inlet or somewhere else. You'd have never even met the girl."

I must have been here too long already today; that statement almost sounded like it made sense. Granted, Bill *had* told me about Mallard Cove after my slip rent skyrocketed over at Lynnhaven, and I had begun looking for a new home base. This was right about the time that Kari had been brought in by the new investor group to redesign and redevelop the Mallard Cove property, so he kind of had a point. And except for beer, he didn't ask me for much.

"Okay fine, Bill. Just write the note, and I'll tape it up when I get back."

Baloney grinned triumphantly, "You're a good man, Shaker. Remember, not a word about it though."

I nodded. "I got it, Bill, the story is all yours."

Back at Mallard Cove, I taped up the note like I had promised. It read: "Guys, meet me over on the slab at Carlton Albury's at quarter to five. Beer's on me today. – Bill"

I was just about to step back when from behind me I heard a very familiar voice. "What's this mystery all about?"

Turning around, I found myself looking into a pair of beautiful hazel eyes, and an equally beautiful but inquisitive smile. Kari.

"I can't tell you." I loved pulling the whole *I know something you don't know* act.

"Why not?"

"Because Bill made me promise to keep quiet."

She put her arms around me and leaned back, cocking her head slightly, her long black hair spilling down to the middle of her back as she asked, "Well, is Bill offering to buy you lunch?" Kari's smile had now morphed into more of a sly one. She's as cunning and smart as she is pretty.

"Just beer, like the note says. But I get your point." While I liked knowing something that she didn't, culinary bribery is never overrated. We turned and walked over to the deck of the *Cove Restaurant* that looked out over Mallard Cove's charter boat row, grabbing a table with a great view of the marina basin.

24

It was a slightly warm early summer day, so the glass-windowed garage doors that separated the deck and the dining room area were open. We were having an early lunch, but the *Cove* was already well on its way to being crowded. Since it was Friday, I was hoping this was an indication of yet another busy Mallard Cove weekend for all of us.

"So, what's the big secret?"

I explained what Baloney was up to. I didn't know exactly what reaction to expect from Kari, but this wasn't it.

"He might have something, Marlin. Charter anglers spend most of their time in the cockpit, and if his looks the same as any new Viking, who cares if the interior isn't as fancy. Sounds like *My Mahi* will be a good addition to the fleet."

I had to concede these points. "At least he has Carlton giving him advice. He'll keep him from getting in too much trouble. You should have seen the two of them standing there, staring up at the hull. I swear it was like they both were seeing it finished."

"They probably were. And speaking of finished, are we still on schedule for tomorrow's launch? I want to invite a few people over tomorrow afternoon to see *Tied Knot*. How would you feel about breaking in the grill up on the sundeck?"

I knew this could easily go from a few people to much of the dock in short order. I'm more of a low key person, and Kari is too, most of the time. But I knew she was really proud of *Tied Knot*, especially since we designed it together. And I also knew who at least two of those folks on the guest list would be. Her parents.

I've gotten along well with her mom on the handful of times that I've met her, but as his favorite daughter, her dad had always hoped Kari would marry some professional guy. He used to have one son in law who was a waterman, working the Chesapeake fishing for crabs, oysters, and clams. Then two weeks ago his youngest daughter graduated from high school and immediately eloped with her boyfriend who is a sportfishing mate, doubling the waterman son in law count. Her parents weren't thrilled about it. And her dad still isn't happy with me, either, partly because I'm seven years older than Kari's twenty-five. It also doesn't help that we can't legally tell them about settlements each of us received related to something that happened with *Why Knot*. I also can't tell them much about the creation of MAFF and how I became the executive director, which was all part of one of those stories from another day. I'm pretty sure her dad thinks that Kari is paying for *Tied Knot* all by herself, since she has that well-paying and highly visible position with M & S. In his mind I'm some kind of a boat bum who is mooching off of her. The truth was that neither she nor I have to work; we're both financially set. But we work because we both love what we are doing.

I saw that I had taken too long before answering, and Kari was now pensively biting her lower lip. I smiled and said, "I'd love to break in the grill. In fact, why don't you invite all of your family to come too. Let's make a real party out of it." I could see the instant relief on her face.

"That would be great! Maybe you can show my dad your boats and the MAFF offices, then he could get a better idea of what you do."

My only interactions with her parents had been at their home on just a few occasions. They had only visited Mallard Cove a couple of times when Kari had first started working on the project. But they hadn't been back since her father learned that she was living with me aboard my vintage Chris Craft. He refers to it as "that deathtrap" because it had exploded back when it had gas engines. The truth was that it didn't go "boom" by itself; it had help. And soon after that, I had it converted to diesel, a much safer alternative.

"Not a bad idea." I didn't really believe that, but the truth was the idea of spending time with her dad made me nervous, but I'd do anything for this woman. This includes hanging out with her father if I have to, though frankly, that wasn't my idea of fun. I knew it wouldn't be high on his list, either. Fortunately, my phone rang just then, leaving this conversation at a good stopping point. I looked at the screen and was surprised but happy with what I saw.

"Captain Albright! What's new and improved?" Greg Albright was the captain of the *Helena Mary*, a vintage ninety-two-foot former US presidential yacht. He and I went back all the way to elementary school together in Richmond, and he had tied up here overnight a few weeks ago on his way up to Massachusetts, giving us a chance to catch up.

"Hey there, Marlin. You mentioned something when I was down there about wanting a fifty-four Irwin ketch. Have you found one yet?" Straight, and to the point. Part of why I liked Greg.

"Not yet."

"Well, I'm looking across the harbor here in Manchester, Massachusetts at one that's out on a mooring. Got a broker's sign on the rail. It's all set up as a 'headboat' with all the Coast Guard equipment and high side railings. Let me text you some pictures."

My phone vibrated as the pictures arrived. I pulled them up and quickly looked them over. "That's exactly what I'm looking for, Greg. Good eye." Fifty-fours were as rare as hen's teeth. I had sailed on one in the Florida Keys, and it was a perfect headboat.

Greg said, "I haven't been aboard her, but she looks good from the channel. Though you know how that goes, especially one that's over twenty years old."

"I do. Hey, thanks for the heads up, I'll call that boat broker. If I come up to look her over, I'll give you a call." If this panned out, I was going to owe Greg, big time.

"Sounds good. I'll be up here for another couple of weeks before heading back to Florida, so if I can help, just give me a call."

"Will do, thanks. I appreciate the lead." I hung up and looked over at Kari.

"Find your unicorn?" Kari had been amused at how insistent I've been on wanting this one particular model of sailboat. Okay, you might even say I've been stubborn about it. Obsessed might be a tad too strong a word. Or, not.

I nodded, "Maybe. Greg Albright saw this one out on a mooring up in Massachusetts. Since it's in the "cheap slips" instead of at a dock, maybe they're squeezed for cash and seriously looking to make a deal. No way they've been getting any casual lookers with it out there." I passed my phone over with the photos.

Kari studied the images. "Doesn't look too bad. Worth a call, anyway."

I agreed with a nod. "Which is what I'm going to do after lunch. But no more business talk until then, I just want to have a quiet and relaxing lunch with you in the meantime."

Kari beamed, handing back my phone after switching the ringer off as she did the same thing with hers.

*****

At that same moment in the production offices of *Tuna Hunters* up in Galax, Massachusetts, Carrington Stuart looked around a room filled with concerned faces. He knew what he was about to tell them wasn't going to help things, but they all had to be kept up to date. As the cast and production crew of *Tuna Hunters*, the future of this group hinged on the show continuing. And as the Senior Producer of the show, now that Lorne was gone, it was all left in the hands of this six foot two inch burly Texan, who was more comfortable with the actual filming side of the show. Contracts, compensation, and all the business dealings had been in Lorne's wheelhouse.

"Hi, guys. I wish I had better news to report but as of right now, the executor of Lorne's estate still hasn't found a buyer for *Tuna Hunters*. I don't need to tell y'all what a unique and rare person Lorne was, and that he left some huge shoes for someone to fill. But so far they haven't found anybody who has the fishing, television, and creative background who is also willing to risk an eight-figure bankroll to buy and continue to produce the show.

"As y'all know, Lorne's death couldn't have come at a worse time for the show. He was still trying to nail down the location contract, and we were already running out of time for that as it was. So, unless the estate can find a buyer in the next few weeks who can also get a location agreement done, we can kiss this next season goodbye. And if we have to skip a year, well, I doubt we'd get picked up. There's just too much competition sitting on the sidelines out there waiting for a crack at our time slot."

Carrington saw the realization dawn on the dozens of faces before him. While it had been in the backs of all their minds since hearing about Lorne's death, none had dared put this nightmare into words, hoping against hope that it wouldn't come to be. Losing Lorne had been a tremendous shock to all of them, but now everyone in the room was facing the loss of their jobs on top of it. The captains and crews of the boats had become dependent on what had originally been supplemental income, but had quickly morphed into their primary income source, and now it was almost certainly gone.

In their defense, the show had been such a huge success and it hadn't shown any signs of slowing down. With that in mind, new boats, along with vehicles and houses, had been purchased by several of the cast. They

29

had all been so confident in that income stream continuing, at least for another few years. For many, this would now become a total financial disaster, forcing fire sales of assets. But not for someone in the room; the person who had set it all in motion. The one that had planned and dreamed of this day for more than a year. Someone who wanted it all stopped, no matter what the cost would be to the others and who had been willing to commit murder to accomplish it. Because so many in the room right then had not given a damn about what it had cost anyone else, they were just out for themselves. Now, they were getting a taste of their own medicine.

Chapter 3

Rather than take all our cars, the bulk of the Beer Thirty Bunch hopped aboard *High Flier* which had already made its last parasail run of the afternoon. Fifteen minutes later I steered us into the cut that runs back through the marsh mud flats and to Albury's Boatyard. We tied up at the travelift slip where Baloney was waiting. I hadn't explained anything to anyone except Kari, so they were all still curious about the venue change and Bill's sudden onset of liquid generosity.

"About time you guys got here. I wanted you to come over so I could show you my new rig!" He led us all over toward the Viking where Kim "Hard Rock" Collier came to a sudden stop.

"Are you kidding me, Baloney? You bought that thing? Just two outboards on that big heavy sumbitch?" Hard Rock thought Baloney must have lost his mind, having bought a pile of junk. Even after Bill told him the whole story he still had major doubts. "Those guys should have paid you to take it off their hands."

"Yeah, well, they almost did, Hard Rock." Baloney had now become grumpy, having expected his old friend to see what he saw in this hull.

"Hey guys, sorry I'm late. Hey, cool Viking! But I don't think those outboards are gonna cut it at much over trolling speed. She yours, Bill?" Timmy "Spud" O'Shea, the owner of Spud's Bait Company at Mallard Cove had just tied up his bait boat, *Rum Runner*, behind *High Flier*.

Baloney brightened up after hearing his comments, "Yeah, Spud, thanks. Finally, somebody else who knows value when they see it."

Lindsay and Murph had just finished circling the hull. Murph spoke up, "Those holes in the hull can be repaired, but I want to see the interior."

We all climbed aboard, and I saw that Bill had been hard at work cleaning up the fishing cockpit. It would need some paint, but it was easy to see there was still a good base to work with. The cabin interior, however, was a nightmare. After having been pumped out this morning, it now had a "low tide" smell left behind from the semi-stagnant water of the boatyard's turning basin. Standing in the middle of the now stripped salon space was Jack "The Ripper" Grayson, another member of the Beer Thirty Bunch, and Bill's good friend. Jack was a world-class marine artist who could do unbelievable things with a paintbrush and a canvas, but right now he had a wicked-looking reciprocating saw in his hands, and he was covered in sawdust. Looks like I had been wrong about Bill having been the one that had been hard at work.

Hard Rock grinned, "Looks like you're earning your nickname again, Ripper."

Jack had one of his paintings reproduced as a limited lithograph in Amsterdam. After the last copy was printed, Jack was supposed to destroy the thin metal plates using a knife to lightly scratch through the image while a newspaper photographer took pictures. Unfortunately, Jack's Dutch was about as bad as the printer's English, and he misinterpreted the instructions. Much to the photographer's delight, Jack used the knife to cut all the way through and halfway across the plate before the horrified printer was able to get him to understand what he had meant. So, it was the newspaper that created his nickname, not Baloney. Though Bill made sure that it had stuck.

"Oh, and I guess you guys thought that beer Bill bought was supposed to be free, huh? All of the cabinets and woodwork down below has to come out now that it was underwater. When she sank the first time most of it stayed dry because the bow was hung up on the pilings. This time the water finished it all.

Meaning it's now a mold farm and its gotta go." Jack held up the Sawzall.

"I don't mind paying Carlton's guys to make new cabinets, but takin' the old ones out is easy enough for all of us to do." Baloney looked around the salon as he gave us a hopeful grin.

I said, "Well gang, it looks like we aren't getting any beer until we strip out this barge. Let's do it."

A little over an hour later we were all sitting around the cockpit on the covering boards, drinking some well-earned beer. A pile of waterlogged cabinetry pieces lay on the ground behind the transom.

"Thanks, guys. Now I can get to work on the engine room myself while the new interior gets built. This was a big help." Baloney was as sincere as he gets, and I realized why. It wasn't just about getting the interior stripped out, it was that he had taken a huge leap of faith with this project. I figured he was going to have most if not all of his savings tied up in it, and he needed the moral support of knowing that we were all behind him. Probably some additional muscle power from all of us too, from time to time.

"You're a jackass, you know that, right? You didn't need to bribe us with beer, Baloney, all you had to do was ask and every one of us would have still showed up, beer or no beer." Spud punched him in the shoulder.

Bill looked embarrassed for a moment then grinned. "Yeah, maybe I am. But I don't ever forget a favor. And Spud, if I don't teach you anything else, remember my number one rule: never turn down free beer!"

I looked at Kari, who was chuckling at Baloney's joke. At least I think it was a joke. But seriously, I knew that part of why Bill had decided to take this risk was he believed in Kari's dedication to making Mallard Cove into ESVA's charter fishing capital. It was already well on its way, and with Bill's determination, I knew *My Mahi* would without a doubt write a great chapter or two in the story about it.

The next morning found Kari and me back at Carlton's, having ridden over there with Baloney. As he headed for *My Mahi,* we climbed aboard *Tied Knot,* which was already positioned on the ways and ready to launch. We tossed lines from both the bow and stern over to Carlton and some of his yard crew who were stationed on the ways' catwalks that run down each side. They took up the slack as the ways slowly started down its steel rails toward the water after Kari broke the traditional bottle of beer over the bow. Okay, Champagne would've been more traditional, but Baloney supplied the bottle and we were keeping with his number one rule. And he was watching from the seawall.

A minute later we were floating, and KT Williams was attaching his towline to the shovel-nosed bow of *Tied Knot.* As he slowly pulled us out from the ways, his brother Junior tucked in behind us, tying his bow up tight against our stern, using his classic deadrise boat more like a rudder than a push boat. We carefully made our way east out through the channel and into Magothy Bay, turning south toward Skidmore Island and the Virginia Inside Passage, five miles ahead.

An hour later the Williams' carefully nudged *Tied Knot* back into her slip as we made her fast to the floating dock's cleats with brand new lines. Shore power, water, pump out and cable lines were all connected next, and then our new home was cooling down inside and ready for us to move in. We spent the next hour checking over every pressure water line as well as the bilges for any leaks before hauling over all of our gear from *Why Knot.* Then Kari and I were off to the grocery store to load up for the party.

"Shaker, this came out beautiful." I wasn't sure if Baloney was talking about the burger on the plate in front of him or *Tied Knot*. In either case, since it came from him, the compliment was delivered in that thick New Jersey accent. I still get a kick out of hearing it and that it hasn't faded much throughout the twenty years that he's lived on ESVA. I hope that never changes.

"Thanks, Bill. We're really happy, and I think this top deck will get a lot of use up until winter." He and I were sitting off by ourselves because most of the other seats on the deck had been taken by the time he and I finished grilling. It was a capacity crowd and we'd gone through a huge pile of burgers and franks.

"Yeah, nice for entertainin'. Carlton's guys did a nice job building her. Seeing how she came together was part of what made me want to take on the Viking. That, and the fact Vikings are built in Jersey."

I laughed, "Yeah, there's that. If they only still made trucks in New Jersey, you'd be all set."

"Yeah, they used to, back in the good old days. We'll see, you just never know what might happen in the future." He grinned at the thought, then turned serious. "About the future, I'm taking a real chance with *My Mahi*, Shaker. She's gonna eat up everything I've got in the bank before she hits the water, which should be this fall. I'm gonna miss everything but rockfish season, and now I just found out they're closing that this year, letting the fishery build back up. I hope I haven't screwed up everything for Betty and me, risking our savings like this."

Bill was headed to the same place I had found myself a year ago, short on cash and long on boats. Back then I was the only one running both of mine, but at least he has B2 on the *Dolphin* to keep some money coming in. I already figured on helping him with finishing the Viking whenever I could when he needed an extra hand.

"Don't worry, Bill. I think you'll look back on this in a few years as one of the best moves you ever made." At least I hoped he would. I saw him brighten as he looked up; Betty was walking over with Kari. Married for over two decades, he still looked at his wife like a high school boy with his first crush.

"Hey guys, what's with the serious talk? Did you happen to notice that there's a party going on around here!" Kari was the happiest that I'd seen her. Having her whole family over had been a great move. They loved *Tied Knot*; it even passed her father's inspection. The jury was still out on me though, as far as he was concerned. But having seen Kari's huge smile as she led her parents, sisters, and brothers in law on a tour was worth putting up with any snub from him. The four of us waded back into the mix that now numbered over two dozen friends and family. It looked like our party deck was going to be the new gathering place during the season when the *Captain's Lounge* and the *Cove Beach Bar* were busy. Even though I liked my privacy, I was still up for it.

The last guest finally left sometime after ten, then Kari and I got a chance to relax and have a last drink by ourselves in the salon before turning in. She could see that something was bothering me.

"What's wrong? Did my dad say something?" She looked worried.

I shook my head. "No, in fact, we hardly spoke at all. It's Bill. He told me that he's putting everything he and Betty have saved into the new boat. It will be ready just in time for the fall rockfish run, but now that fishery will be closed this year, so the boat won't be going out regularly until spring. That's a long time with no income and having nothing left in the bank."

"Can we loan them some cash to get through it?" Kari was now as worried about our friends as I was.

"I doubt he'd take it; you know how Bill is. No, I don't know what we can do other than lend a hand with the rebuild whenever we have spare time."

Kari bit her lower lip; her "tell" whenever she's really worried. "That's what we'll do then. That, plus keeping an eye out for any way that we can send them business in the downtime."

I nodded. Unfortunately, I didn't see any other options at this point. But I knew that we both would try to think of something.

Chapter 4

I woke up a little before five, a little light from the false dawn coming in through the windows. As usual, Kari was already wide awake and looking at me.

"Hey." God, how I loved her voice, especially in the early morning. The way that she said that one word was beyond sexy.

"Hey yourself." I hoped I knew where this was heading. Again. Last night we discovered that we liked all the space in our new bed, if you catch my drift.

"I was thinking about what you said last night about Bill and Betty." This wasn't where I had hoped the conversation was headed, but it was important. "Do you think you can find something for him to do at MAFF until spring?"

I sighed, partially in disappointment, and partially out of frustration because I had been thinking the same thing. But I knew Bill wouldn't take a "busy work" job; he'd see through it as charity, and that wouldn't sit well with him.

"Could I? Yes. Would he? No." Taking free beer from everyone is one thing, especially since up until now he could afford his own. But he wouldn't ever want to be regarded as someone who needed to live off the charity of others. Especially when he would own two charter boats that together will make him a very good living once the busy season started next spring.

Kari's head was on my arm, and in the dim light, I felt rather than saw her head nod. "I suppose you're right."

"Trust me. But things have a way of working out, and the best thing we can do is to stick close to him and help however we can. One way or another, we'll make sure he and Betty get through the slow time." While I was worried, I also believed wholeheartedly in what I had just said.

Kari snuggled in closer and put an arm across my chest. At first, I thought it was in silent agreement to what I had said. Instead, it turned out to be a prelude to what I had hoped would happen.

A couple of hours later we found ourselves on the deck of the *Cove Restaurant*, having breakfast while looking out over the marina basin and in the distance the bow of *Tied Knot*. We tried to avoid "screen time" during meals, but I was waiting for a text from the yacht broker in Massachusetts. It finally came in as we were having our last cup of coffee. I sent one of my own after reading it.

"Sorry, but the broker said he could show me the Irwin this afternoon. I just texted Sam Knight to see if he could run me up there in Shaw Air's Aerostar." Sam Knight was the chief pilot of Casey's air charter service, and their Aerostar was a fast piston engine prop plane. I should be able to go up and back for about the price of a first-class ticket and do it in a fraction of the time it would take to fly with the airlines.

"I hope this third one is the charm." Kari was referring to the previous two Irwins that I hadn't been able to make deals for. In those cases, the owners thought their average condition boats were worth a lot more than the average sale price. That happens more often than you might think with boat owners. Usually, after they get a dose of reality, the prices drop down to where they should have been in the first place, but not before the owners have to pony up a lot more in dockage. Money they never got back.

"You and me, both. I want to build up some sailing tour traffic this summer before somebody else gets the same idea to run a 'head boat' out of here. This should round out our charter dock, with something to offer everybody." Just then, I got a text from Sam, "Hey, maybe my luck with Irwins has finally turned. Sam has to pick up a charter in New York at noon in Shaw Air's

Citation jet, so he's deadheading up there today, and he's empty again coming back from there tomorrow afternoon. So, he said that he can haul me to Massachusetts for the same price as it would have cost in the prop plane, but in half the time. The only catch is I'll have to leave now, stay up there overnight, and get picked back up late tomorrow."

"That might not be a bad thing; that way you aren't pushed for time checking out the Irwin," Kari mused.

"I was thinking that, too. If I can make a deal, that also gives me more time to arrange to have her hauled and surveyed. I've got to pack and run right now to make it though."

"Let's get you going."

I called Greg on my drive up to Accomack Airport and scored, big time. Since he had a rental car, he offered me a ride to and from the Beverly Municipal Airport. His boss wasn't due back in town until late next week, so he also invited me to stay aboard the *Helena Mary* tonight. I sure wasn't about to turn down the chance to stay on such a cool part of history. She'd been the yacht of half a dozen US presidents and had even been re-named for the granddaughter of one of them. Since I have loved living aboard my vintage wooden Chris Craft the past several years, you can imagine what a thrill this would be for me, staying on a vintage wooden yacht with such a historic pedigree. It just reinforced the idea that my "Irwin luck" might have started to change. Now all I had to do was make a deal.

Since it was just Sam and me on the trip, I got to ride up front in the co-pilot's seat. It also gave us a chance to chat after we reached altitude and he wasn't as busy. Sam's a cool guy who looks and even sounds like a much younger Sam Elliott, mustache and all. He's flown a ton of different aircraft and has so much experience flying that he could make even the most nervous passenger relax. He and I have a shared love of fishing, which dominated this airborne conversation until we started our descent and his attention turned back to preparing for landing.

Greg was waiting when we walked into the reception area of the local fixed base operation. I introduced the two then said goodbye to Sam as he went to pay the landing fee and arrange for fuel while Greg and I headed for the rental car. After we climbed in, Greg gave me an update.

"A couple of the guys around the docks told me about that sailboat. The couple who own her split up. They had been running it as a tourist operation themselves. They took turns as captain and had a full-time mate. I guess they figured it would be easier if one was always ashore; that way they wouldn't get burned out. Turned out that it was easier all right, easier for her to meet some dude from one of the charters, and easier to screw around while she and the dude were ashore and her partner was out working. Now she's moved in with the charter guy down in Boston. She's forcing her ex to sell the boat and give her half of the money since he doesn't have enough cash to buy her out. Could be some nice leverage there." He glanced my way with a sly grin.

Yep, I was going to owe Greg, big time. "Great info. Yeah, their asking price is a little high even if the boat is in great shape, and I was hoping to be able to get it down a bit. Sounds like I might have a shot at that."

We met the broker at Greg's dock, then rode out to the Irwin's mooring in the guy's Boston Whaler. He was a real pro, telling us to take our time looking her over after he ran us through all her specifications. I had my game face on, trying to look as noncommittal and as slightly disinterested as possible. I could have gotten an Academy Award for my performance; she was exactly what I was looking for and had been well taken care of. The only slight issue I found was some "dock rash" and a few rust streaks and stains on her otherwise white hull, but I planned on having her painted red to match my parasail and eco-tour boats anyway.

I made a lowball offer right then, and the broker went up to the bow to confer with his clients in a conference call. He returned ten minutes later with a counteroffer that was already lower than I expected to have to pay. I could see that he was bracing for a counter from me, and I sensed he was worried. From what little Greg and I had overheard of his conversation from our spot back at the helm, we knew that the owners were the "clients from hell" and he was caught in the middle of a nautical "war of the roses". The relief on his face was obvious when I accepted their counter offer without tossing out another counter of my own. He hadn't looked forward to a prolonged negotiation with the two of them, and I was getting a more than fair price. It was a win/win situation for everybody.

Greg had given me the name of a good marine surveyor that he had gotten from a friend back on the dock. Rule number one when buying a boat: never use the seller's broker's surveyor pal; you want someone who is working just for you. I gave the broker the guy's name, and he wrote up a contract subject to survey, then I wrote out a deposit check. At that point, my elusive unicorn was lassoed and soon would be heading down to my barn.

The broker dropped Greg and me back at the dock, and we headed to the *Helena Mary* for an early celebratory cocktail on her fantail. She was truly a stunning vessel at ninety–two–feet long, with most of everything above her shearline being either hand-oiled or varnished wood, or chrome-plated metal. I could appreciate her beauty, and also the fact that she was truly a maintenance nightmare. Even though it hadn't been that long since she was at Mallard Cove, I still stopped to take her all in again.

Greg noticed that I was lagging behind, but quickly understood why. He was used to the *Helena Mary* being a show stopper. I was excited about staying aboard tonight, and told Greg that dinner out was on me, with his pick of the restaurant. The grin I got in return told me that it was going to be expensive, but at that point I didn't care. Just finding the Irwin alone was worth that to me, not to mention the overnight accommodations.

We went aboard and Greg had no sooner started building our drinks before a gargantuan guy started up the gangway, followed by an equally large white Labrador retriever. The huge, bearded, biracial man looked to be over six and a half feet tall and was closer to four hundred than three hundred pounds. Dressed in Sportif shorts and a short sleeve Bahama fishing shirt, you could easily see the large tribal tattoos that covered his massive arms from his biceps down to his wrists. Imposing would be one way to describe him, and scary would be another. I hoped that he and Greg were on friendly terms.

"What's an out of work reality show captain got to do to get a drink around here?" The voice didn't match the look at all. If I had to use one word to describe it I'd use "gentle". The voice jogged my memory, and that's when I recognized him as Smitty from *Tuna Hunters*, the reality TV fishing show.

Greg chuckled, "Sit your big butt down in a chair, and try not to break it when you do. Rum and cola?"

"Rum and diet cola. I'm trying to lose weight so you can quit worrying about your darn deck chairs." Before he sat down he reached over with an island sized hand and said, "Hi, I'm Smitty."

I shook his hand, which was probably fifty percent larger than mine. "Yeah, I know. I'm Marlin Denton, it's nice to meet you."

"Oh, hey, you're the guy who's interested in that sailboat. I gave Greg the name of a good surveyor in case you make a deal."

"I did make a deal, and thanks, the broker is getting your guy lined up now." There was something about the combination of Smitty's voice and his imposing frame that made him feel very comfortable to be around. I sat down in a chair next to his.

Greg chimed in, "I met Smitty a few years back, down in Florida. This was before he ever got on television. So, Smitty, we're celebrating Marlin's deal. Dinner's on him tonight, are you in? We're going to Maximillian's." He brought over the drinks and sat in a chair across from me.

"Ah! Maximillian's, 'where you had better bring many millions!' Heck yes, I'm in. I used to not even worry about going to a place as expensive as that one, but now..." His voice trailed off.

Two things hit me about that. First, it confirmed my fears that it was probably the most expensive place in town, and that picking up the tab should square my debt with Greg. That's also why I didn't mind his spontaneous addition of Smitty to our dinner party. But second, it brought back up Smitty's original comment about being "out of work". I was curious, since I had caught the show a few times. I thought it was still popular.

"So, you're leaving the show? I would have thought it was a good gig."

Smitty filled Greg and me in on what had happened with Lorne Gillam's murder, and how earlier in the week the producer had given them the news about the show not finding a buyer.

"Tough to find a buyer. Lorne was like he was born to create this show. He loved television, and with his family background, he understood fishing and fishermen, too. Even now that it's already put together, to keep it successful we'd at least need somebody who knows the water, boats, and fishing to buy it. *And* they'd need to be able to get those politicians down south to come to their senses and sign a deal in the next week or so. Any buyer would need to have really deep pockets to buy the show and be willing to foot the bill to produce the next season before they'd ever see a dime in return. There just doesn't seem to be anybody like that out there." The regret in Smitty's voice hung heavily in the air.

Man, I really hated to see *Tuna Hunters* die, even though I hadn't watched it in a year or so. I prefer reading books to watching television. And yes, it was "reality" television with semi-scripted drama, at least as scripted as a fishing show could ever be. But what had attracted me to it was that it gave millions of people insight into and appreciation of what went into catching that sushi roll they ate at a restaurant, and the hunks of tuna they brought home from the grocery and warehouse club stores. It also touched on why we needed to continue to protect this fishery.

This last point was one that I thought they could've done more with, but I was looking at it from the MAFF viewpoint. Of course, MAFF's main objective is the protection of our mid-Atlantic fisheries, as well as the education of the public as to why this is so important. Through our tournament prize subsidy program, we also support billfish tournaments that are strictly catch and release. And we are moving into not just the protection of more fisheries but raising public awareness about sustainable fishing methods and the importance of supporting independent fishermen such as the watermen of ESVA.

This was the point where the light bulb came on over my head. I excused myself for a few minutes, leaving Greg and Smitty to chat while I went into the privacy of the salon to make a few calls. When I came back about ten minutes later I addressed Smitty.

"*Tuna Hunter*'s producer must live close by, right?"

"Down in Galax, about fifteen minutes from here, why?" Smitty looked curious.

"Call him up and tell him that I'd like to meet with him."

"About what, Marlin?"

"Buying *Tuna Hunters.*"

Smitty laughed out loud before he caught himself. Apparently, I didn't look the part of someone he thought of as a being a potential buyer for the show. He looked both embarrassed and apologetic as he said, "Marlin, I think you missed the bit about it costing somewhere well into the eight-figure range to buy it and produce a season. There's a big difference between being able to buy an old sailboat and buying a television show."

Greg jumped in after first giving me an amazed look, "Smitty, I told you that I picked Marlin up at the airport, but I didn't tell you that he came in on a private jet. If he thinks he can afford to buy it, then I believe him." He gave me a hard look and said, "You *can* afford it, right Marlin?"

"The foundation I'm involved with is a ready, willing, and capable buyer with cash in hand." I could see that Smitty wasn't convinced yet, and I doubted he'd make the call until he was darn sure that I was what I claimed to be.

"Marlin, what do you know about television? This is a competitive business, and we're talking about some huge numbers. And we still don't have a deal with that town in the Carolinas." Smitty had budged a bit, but he wasn't there yet.

"I'm hoping that your producer knows all we need to cover the television production side of the business, which is part of what I want to find out when we meet. And all together my foundation board has a greater depth of business knowledge than most. Plus, I just got a verbal agreement from the head of the county board of supervisors at the show's new location on Virginia's Eastern Shore. They'd love the publicity this will bring."

"What about the fishing? Without tuna, there's no show." Smitty sounded skeptical, as if the Carolina location was the only decent mid-Atlantic tuna fishing in the early season.

"Those same fish come past Virginia, too. The fishing grounds are not quite as narrow, meaning you have to work a little harder, but we still get them. Richlands Seafood over at Newport News Seafood Harbor buys bluefin all season long, and they pay well. I don't think we'll have a problem getting a truck to pick them up over at Mallard Cove Marina."

Smitty was starting to lean a bit farther in my direction, but he still wasn't totally convinced. "What about the Carolina fleet? You'll have to negotiate with them to come up to Virginia; they're as stubborn as their politicians."

"I know some folks in ESVA that would love to have their spots, and many of them are just as crazy if not more so than those Carolina crews. So trust me, we can replace them with a colorful cast of ESVA characters. Those Carolina crews should have already brought pressure on their politicians to make a deal with you guys, but they didn't. Why not be where you are wanted and appreciated by everybody? So, invite your producer over so we can talk. If we're going to make a deal and get this show back on track, it sounds like there's no time to waste."

With a sideways glance at Greg, Smitty begrudgingly pulled out his phone and hit a preprogrammed number. "Carrington? You need to come up to Jonas' Wharf in Manchester. There's somebody here you need to meet. He might just be a buyer for the show."

Chapter 5

Our conversation extended well into my regular dinner time. We all loaded up and headed out to eat after dropping off Smitty's four-pawed pal on his boat, which was docked a few slips over from Greg. By the time we arrived at the restaurant, Carrington and I had already developed a mutual respect and decided we could work well together. We each had strong points that complimented the other's. However, after hearing from him the executor's asking price, I knew I could get it cheaper. Much cheaper. Yes, the foundation has a huge endowment and we could meet that price, but that also didn't mean we should be stupid and retail. And while I might not know about camera angles or editing, I do know a thing or two about leverage.

Face it, the estate hadn't had the first offer yet, and they had just days before everything but the rights to the prior season's shows became worthless. If they were going to salvage anything out of this ongoing part of the franchise, I was their only hope. Another thing in my favor was that without an ongoing show, the syndication value of the older episodes would drastically diminish in short order. I decided on my first offer before we left for the restaurant, and Carrington passed it along. The executor made a counteroffer by the time we had dessert. After coffee, I made my counter that was a "drop dead" figure with an expiration of tomorrow at ten a.m.

We didn't hear anything more as the executor must've decided to sleep on my offer overnight. But it had become one of the most interesting dinners of my life. I liked what I was now seeing on the faces of both Carrington and Smitty; it was cautious optimism, a real turnaround from where they had both been when we met.

The four of us gathered the next morning a little before nine at a great little "locals" breakfast place that Smitty knew. We had just been seated when I got the call. The executor tried one more time to get me to come up on the price. I asked him if he didn't fully understand the concept of a "drop dead" offer and told him we had nothing further to talk about. I saw the stunned faces across the table right before I winked. A few seconds later he caved, and MAFF now had another potential income source. But even more importantly, we now had another great educational tool that would reach far beyond just the mid-Atlantic.

Carrington sent out a text setting up a crew meeting for eleven o'clock today down at the production office in Galax, less than a half-hour drive from the restaurant. He didn't list a reason other than it was an "all call". This meant that attendance was mandatory, and everyone would get paid for their time. The tension in the room when we walked in was palpable. No one there knew if this was to announce the show had officially folded and that it would be the last time they'd all be together as one group. Carrington had deliberately waited until now before explaining the deal and announcing the cast and location changes while I was standing alongside him to be introduced and to answer their questions. Waiting until that moment had been his call; he wanted to emphasize my part in the show's business side from this point on.

To say that it was an emotional meeting would be selling it way too short. When he announced the show had sold, the burst of relief they all shared was overwhelming. I was getting looks that were made up of equal parts of gratitude and curiosity. After Carrington announced the new location, their curiosity ratcheted up even farther. A few fiddled with their smartphones, looking up the area. Like so many other people on the Eastern Seaboard, the folks at *Tuna Hunters* were mostly clueless about ESVA. It's like there's a gap that exists on the nautical charts between Ocean City, Maryland, and Virginia Beach.

Admittedly, the Chesapeake side of both Virginia and Maryland's Eastern Shore is much better known, due mostly to the summer influx of Washington, DC's movers and shakers that either visit or own homes there. There are only a few decent harbors on the southern Atlantic side of the shared peninsula, and many of their inlets can be tough to navigate. The barrier islands that border these inlets are mostly marsh, sand and scrub, with the only access being by shallow draft boat. But being so undeveloped is a big part of the charm of this part of the world, at least from my perspective.

We needed to move fast now to get everything in place before the deal was officially announced. So, everyone left after the meeting with individual assignments and also sworn to secrecy. They were also still somewhat curious about both me and ESVA but elated too. Well, not quite everyone was elated, but I wouldn't find that part out until later. Meanwhile, there was also a ton of work to be done back in ESVA. I had to meet with the foundation's attorneys tomorrow and set up the closing for the purchase, get a new contract in place with the cable channel that would air us, as well as get all of our local permits all in hand. Plus, we had to get new location offices established back at Mallard Cove.

All of this was going to take people with expertise, and fortunately, we had them already in place on the show's staff according to Carrington. Plus, MAFF has a ton of spare room on our floor of the Mallard Cove office building, so we could get set up there asap. I was bringing both Carrington and Smitty back down with me in the plane this afternoon, along with Smitty's lab, Thor. Carrington knew who on the staff was needed where, and Smitty was more or less a cast liaison as well as being one of the most popular cast members, having been with the show since day one. Everyone liked and respected him, and after replacing the Carolina crews, we couldn't afford to lose any of our original New England cast. He would be perfect as a go-between. Ultimately though, the new cast member choices would be left up to Carrington, but he respected Smitty's opinion. I had a good list of local prospects I wanted them to meet, starting of course with Baloney.

Okay, I admit it, helping Bill was one of the reasons I wanted MAFF to buy the *Tuna Hunters* show. But certainly not the main reason. Though by now you've gotten a good look at Baloney, and you know that if there ever was a character who was born to star in a cable fishing reality show, Bill is that guy. When I described him and told them the story of his new boat, I piqued Carrington and Smitty's interests. Though I think they thought I was exaggerating about what a character he is. They were both in for a surprise; I had downplayed that part.

Until we nailed down our ESVA based cast members, we were keeping everything completely quiet down there about both the purchase and the move. I needed these two to meet the prospective cast members and see them as they are, not as they might want to be seen to get a part. We concocted a story about the three of us having been old fishing friends, and how I ran into them when Carrington was visiting Smitty up north. I was bringing them back to ESVA so we could get in some white marlin fishing, since we were already well into the summer run. It would allow them to blend in with the Beer Thirty Bunch and the other locals without raising any suspicions. Now we headed for the airport since I was anxious to get back to ESVA and get to work.

*****

Damn it! This wasn't supposed to have happened. There shouldn't have been any buyers for the show; it should have died, just as that bloodsucker Lorne had. Killing was so final, so permanent, but sometimes there was no other choice when people just couldn't take a hint. Hopefully it won't come to that again, but if it does, so be it. But only as a last resort. Right now there are other ways to save people from themselves. Time to try to steer this ship onto the rocks. Again.

*****

At the airport and I introduced Carrington, Smitty, and Thor to Sam, whose eyes grew a little wide as he took in the size of Smitty. As I said, Carrington is a big guy in his own right, but Smitty was in a class all by himself. Seeing Smitty squeeze through the doorway of the Citation reminded me a bit like putting the cork back in a bottle of wine. Then down at the airport in ESVA, the four of us loading into my vintage Explorer Sport Trac was another grand adventure. Smitty barely fit in the front passenger seat and left zero legroom behind him. Thor lay crosswise on Smitty's side of the back seat, or at least mostly on that side. Carrington managed to wedge himself in behind me and had Thor's head in his lap, but fortunately, we only had less than an hour to drive. I mentally added another thing to tomorrow's "to do" list; leasing one of those Sprinter touring vans that had plenty of leg and headroom.

As we drove down US 13, I could see the disappointment on both of their faces. I guess they were expecting views of the water from our main drag like there are down in the Florida Keys. Instead, what they saw were farm fields, woods, and dozens of long low metal buildings that each housed thousands of chickens. The thing is, no matter where you are on 13, you're no farther than five miles from the water on either side. But despite how flat and narrow ESVA is,

52

the view they were seeing could have been in any agricultural area of the country. US 13, our main road, only comes within sight of the water at the southern tip of this five to twelve-mile wide peninsula. That tip is exactly where Mallard Cove is located.

"Guys, don't worry, it gets more scenic up ahead, I swear." It didn't look like I was being too convincing. That changed when we turned in to the Mallard Cove property.

"Holy crap! You weren't kidding. This place looks like it was built just for the show." Smitty's doubts were erased now.

I could see Carrington was also absorbing the setting, no doubt already figuring out the best backdrops for different shots.

"Can we use the boat forklift at that in and out storage for lifting the tuna out of the boats? It's big and dramatic looking with those long forks. We can set up the fish buyer's truck down there and have that boat barn in the background."

"Whatever you need." I was glad he was already "into" the location.

He pointed over to the right toward the marina basin inlet. "What a great shot that'll be; looking straight down the inlet with that island and those long bridges on the right, and the ocean out in the distance on the left with the boats coming and going. You weren't kidding; it is picturesque. You had me worried on the ride down."

I chuckled. "If it wasn't a cool looking place, there wouldn't have been any point in having the show here. But it will be a great location and the publicity will be good for Mallard Cove. Everybody wins."

We parked and grabbed our gear, walking down the west dock past charter boat row on the left, and the *Cove Restaurant's* deck to our right. The glass-paneled garage doors of the dining room were up, and a guitar duo was playing out on the deck. Even though it was late on a Sunday afternoon, the place was still packed. It's usually like that in the summer.

Smitty commented, "Cool looking place. How's the food?"

"As good or better than Maximillian's, and without the hefty price tag." Even if my friends and fiancée hadn't owned it, the *Cove* would still be my favorite place, followed closely by the *Fin and Steak*, the other restaurant they owned here at Mallard Cove.

"I think this could be the beginning of a beautiful friendship." Smitty did a great Bogart imitation, with a huge grin on his face. Mallard Cove already appealed to him.

Carrington was still in his initial assessment mode, looking over the marina basin from all angles, lost in his own world. Finally, he turned and said what I really (eliminate "really") had hoped to hear: "This place will work so much better than the one we were working out of in Carolina. Now, if only the fishing is as good."

"Like I said, we get the same tuna schools that pass through Carolina. They all spawn in the Gulf of Mexico, and they have to go past here to get to their northern feeding grounds. If you're good, you can do well here."

We made the left turn down to the private dock and passed through the security gate. Once we got to *Tied Knot*, I introduced them both to Kari, then showed them to our two guest staterooms. Then all four of us headed up to the top deck where Murph and Lindsay were already sitting at the bar. Murph is a few years older than me, but about my same height with shaggy brown hair. Lindsay is a year older than Kari, and her same height but with long blonde hair and the look of someone who loves being outdoors.

"I figured you guys already had a full day of it, and we could relax up here and grill out," Kari explained. Then she introduced them to Murph and Lindsay who, because of their being MAFF board members, already knew what was going on with *Tuna Hunters.* She filled Carrington and Smitty in on their background with Mallard Cove and *Irish Luck,* plus the fact that they're our best friends.

"What's a guy got to do to get a beer around here?" Baloney had come up from the dock via the aft stairs.

"You know where they're kept, Baloney," I replied.

"Yeah, I do, but they taste better when you hand 'em to me. Hey, who are you two? Ya know, you look a lot like that guy on that tuna show."

"That's because he *is* that guy from the tuna show. Smitty, Carrington, meet Captain Bill "Baloney" Cooper. Or, as we're going to start calling him, 'Commodore'. He owns the *Golden Dolphin* over in the corner, and *My Mahi,* which is 'up on the hard' right now. Bill, these guys are old fishing pals of mine, just down for a bit of a vacation and to catch a few billfish."

"Well hey, any friend of Shaker here is okay in my book. Yeah, Smitty, I've caught your show a bunch of times. I gotta say though, you guys sure talk a lot when you fish."

Smitty glanced at Carrington then at me as if to silently ask, "Is this guy for real?" He smiled at Bill and said, "Yeah, but if we didn't, it'd be a really boring show. During my first episode, I kept getting notes from the director telling me to talk more and pretend that I was explaining tuna fishing to a bunch of young kids. Almost none of our audience has ever been out fishing offshore, much less ever seen a tuna that wasn't in a sushi roll. They don't get the fact that a big tuna is the size of a Volkswagen and can weigh almost as much. You know that even the biggest flat screen TV can never get across what catching tuna is like in real life, and it's our job to get viewers to understand it."

Baloney nodded thoughtfully. "You're right about that; I guess I never looked at it that way before. When you live to fish, it's easy to forget that the rest of the world doesn't know what you do. Course, most of this marina don't know either, present company excepted. We've got more than our share of weekend warriors here." He grinned as his ever-present and unlit cigar slowly swapped sides in his mouth.

Bill's wife Betty showed up a few minutes later, and despite her best efforts to reign him in a bit Baloney was in rare form, telling Smitty and Carrington his favorite fishing stories. They both got along great with him, like they were all lifelong friends. The stories got wilder and more colorful as the sun, drinks and food all went down. I saw Carrington and Smitty quickly huddling over in a corner, then they beckoned to me.

Carrington said in a low voice, "He's perfect. Let's sign him up." Smitty nodded his head in agreement.

I went over and sat in the unoccupied chair next to Bill. "Hey, Baloney, you think you can have your new 'boatyard ornament' ready to go by December?"

Bill shot me an irritated glance. "She'll be ready to go alright, not that there's much of anybody around that wants to go fishing for anything but rockfish then. Bunch of cold weather wimps. But seeing Smitty here has given me an idea, maybe I'll go after tuna and sell 'em commercially instead of chartering then."

"How would you like to keep her running daily from December through February?"

He looked at me like I was daft. "That's what I'm talking about, Shaker, me and B2 keeping her bringing in cash through part of the winter."

"What would you think about bringing a camera person along with you?" I couldn't help it; I was now enjoying the confused look on his face since I knew what was coming up next.

"Whatta you mean, bring a camera person?"

Now Carrington jumped into the conversation. "Bill, I haven't been completely straight with you. I'm the producer of *Tuna Hunters*. Smitty and I are down here because the show is moving to Mallard Cove, and we are putting together a new southern fleet for the show. Marlin suggested you as the first candidate, and we think you'd be perfect."

Bill and Betty both looked stunned, then she reached over and grabbed his hand. They both realized this could be the lifeboat they desperately needed right now. Bill recovered quickly then asked, "So, what's it pay?"

"We'll start you at ten thousand per episode for your boat. The percentage you give your mate out of that is up to you."

"Ten grand! Wow, that's great! Wait, you said 'per episode' not per season? How many episodes in a season?" Bill was trying to absorb it all as fast as he could.

"Sixteen episodes."

It was a good thing that Bill was sitting down at that point. I saw Betty now unconsciously crushing his hand as she did the math in her head. Their lifeboat had just become a megayacht. Bill recovered quickly and had a ton of questions.

"I still get to keep the money for the tuna, right?"

Carrington smiled. "Of course."

"I get to pick my own mate?"

"Our deal is with you, and your crew is your own business. So unless it's someone who doesn't work well on TV, you can pick your own mate or mates."

"I'm gonna need some new gear and stuff. You guys pay for that?"

Carrington glanced my way and winked. "You have to supply your own after-show beer, Baloney. But you'll be getting a lot of offers from fishing gear suppliers for free gear or sponsorships. You watch the show, so you've seen the stickers around the helms and on the back bulkheads, the decks, and even the logos on the crew's shirts. Those companies all pay them for those placements. So, you won't have to worry about buying gear, they'll be knocking down your door. And many of the crews also receive nice personal appearance fees in the off-season, not to mention the increase in their charter rates and bookings."

Bill and Betty looked at each other, their eyes saying more right then than their voices ever could. Bill turned back to Carrington, "You said that Marlin suggested me?"

"Marlin is now the executive producer of the show."

"What? Since when?"

It was my turn to speak up again. "Since MAFF bought *Tuna Hunters* this morning. We're going to use it as an educational tool, as well as for income."

Bill shook his head. It was one of those very rare times when he was at a loss for words. It didn't last long. "Hey Marlin, whatta you bet I can get a beer company to buy a spot on my Dolphin Fleet tee shirts now? Maybe I can even get them to throw some free beer into the deal!"

Everyone laughed, then came over to congratulate Bill and Betty after I shook hands with him. Done deal.

Smitty's phone rang, and he peeled away from the group. "What? How far did she go down? Are you sure? Any idea who did it? You need me to come back right away? Okay, stay close, and you watch your ass. Call me if you find out anything more." He looked up and saw we had all stopped talking and were now staring at him. "Somebody just tried to scuttle my boat. Luckily my mate was staying aboard and saw she was already low in the water when he came back from picking up dinner. Got some big dewatering pumps going and stopped her from sinking. The engine and generator didn't even go under. But whoever it was had pulled the raw water strainer's sight glass off."

Raw water strainers are attached to the through-hull intakes for the engine cooling water and catch anything like seaweed that might damage or clog the system. I said, "Maybe it just vibrated loose."

Smitty shook his head. "Not unless the bilge pump wires vibrated off the battery posts at the same time, and the high water alarms smashed themselves. No, this was somebody who knew boats really well." He looked at Bill, "There are a few downsides to being on the show, and this is one of them. Other crews get jealous, and then there's the occasional wacko. It just goes with the territory, though this is the first time that anybody has tried sinking me."

*****

I can't catch a frigging break! I thought he was going out for dinner, not just picking up takeout. Another ten minutes and she'd have been low enough for the water to reach the cockpit deck, then they couldn't have stopped it before she was under. Now I need another plan. Maybe I'm looking in the wrong direction. I'll have to figure out something else.

Chapter 6

The next morning the four of us on *Tied Knot* grabbed breakfast at the *Cove* and headed over to the office with Thor in tow. We all got off the elevator on the second floor and went into the MAFF office. I introduced Carrington and Smitty to Sharon Dee Albury, Kari's distant cousin and my chief staff member at MAFF. At a distance, Sharon and Kari could almost pass for twins except for the fact her eyes were green and she was seven years older. I quickly brought her up to speed about purchasing *Tuna Hunters* but didn't even need to tell her to keep it in confidence. She's as sharp as they come, and a big part of the reason I could still build my fleet while simultaneously running MAFF. I also asked her to arrange for that Sprinter van.

We all moved over into the huge empty and unfinished space next to my office and Sharon's. After deciding what types of spaces and square footage we'd need, Kari made a rough sketch laying out the walls that would have to be added to create production offices and a big conference room. Then she went to her own office upstairs to arrange for the construction, since her group was also our landlord. The guys and I drove over to Carlton's boatyard to check out Baloney's new boat and get his input on narrowing down our list of potential crews for the show. Nobody in ESVA had a better "finger on the pulse" of all the charter boats and crews around ESVA than Baloney.

We pulled up next to *My Mahi* on the slab, once again looking like a clown car from the circus as we unloaded. That van couldn't get here fast enough. I heard Baloney's laughter coming from up in the fishing cockpit.

"Smitty, you and Tex gotta quit eating if you're gonna keep riding with Shaker!" It was nice to hear Bill back in his old form again. I spotted him up at the gunwale, and he looked like a new man since now he wasn't so concerned about getting through the winter. It's amazing how much stress can age a person, and it was great to see him lighten up so much, literally overnight.

"Tex?" Carrington didn't realize it yet, but as you're so well aware, getting a nickname from Baloney was the equivalent of being knighted here at Mallard Cove.

"Yeah, Tex! I tried to come up with somethin' for Smitty, but it sounds like somebody already beat me to it."

Carrington looked at me and I just shrugged. He chuckled under his breath and shook his head slightly. Tex it was. The three of us climbed the ladder up into the cockpit while Thor lay down in the shade under the boat.

"Hey, Baloney, you might want to invest in a few giant corks, you've got some holes in your hull." Any concerns I might have had about these two getting along after the new nickname bit had just evaporated. Apparently, "Tex" could hold his own in a head to head matchup with Bill.

"Yeah, well, *you* put a cork in it! When I get done, you'll never know she was holed."

Yep, this was going to be a fun season. I could see that Smitty was thinking the same thing I was as he sat on the aft covering board over the stern with a big grin on his face. Just wait until the rest of the northern fleet gets down here, they were in for a surprise with Bill. The impromptu radio chatter was going to be hilarious, probably the best in *Tuna Hunters* history. I hated to stop these two, but we still had a lot of work to be done, and only a short time in which to do it.

"Okay Bill, we need your input to help pick three more boats and crews to represent the southern fleet. Any ideas?"

"Right off the bat, I'd say Hard Rock and Gaffer would be good. Great fishermen, good boat, and funny as hell. Oops, can I say that on tv?" He had a chastised look.

"Tex" replied, "Say whatever you want, it's not live. We do weeks of editing before a show is ready, and frankly, a few bleeped words are expected and will add some interest. Remember, this is a show about fishing and fishermen, not a televised church service."

"What the heck kind of boats are those?" Smitty was pointing over toward the basin where the Williams' brothers deadrises were now coming into view. Deadrises are the workhorses of the bay waters. KT's headed for the dock next to the travelift slip while Junior pulled into the waiting ways. Junior's was a classic wooden deadrise with a tiny cabin way up in the bow and a huge open but narrow open deck aft. KT's was the more modern version; a much wider fiberglass hull with a larger wheelhouse and smaller open deck that was partially covered by an overhang. His was equipped with outriggers and set up for trolling.

Baloney beat me to the punch, "Those are Chesapeake deadrises, and you'll see a lot of them around here. They first built 'em about the time gas marine engines were invented. Changed a bit as engines got more powerful, but not all that much. You can see from that one they got a little wider, and a bit longer, but that's about it."

"The closer one's hull looks like our Downeaster's, but that other one's cabin is tiny." Smitty looked and sounded skeptical.

"Smitty, to you a megayacht's cabin would feel tiny! And that's a workboat so it don't need a lot of cabin room. They ain't like those party barges you guys got back up north; ours work for a livin' around here." Baloney scoffed.

Smitty's face read "challenge accepted" as he shot back, "Says the man who is rebuilding the floating Taj Mahal."

I whistled and said, "Time out! Save it for the show. Which we won't have unless we can finish picking out the boats and crews and getting them signed up."

"Sorry, Shaker. But these boys are gonna be fun to be around. Especially when I beat Smitty this next year."

"Pack a lunch and bring friends, little guy." Smitty loved a challenge.

"Guys! Let's get back to work. We need some options here." I wanted them to focus, which they finally did. In ten minutes Bill and I had come up with a list of half a dozen potential candidate boats and crews, headed up by the *Kembe II* and Hard Rock. I figured Smitty and "Tex" could get a good look at the Hard Rock and his mate the Mad Gaffer at this afternoon's Beer Thirty Bunch. Then we'd make our way down the list after that.

Just when you have life all figured out and you think you have your ducks all in a row, the Fates can throw a wrench in your plans. But on those rare occasions, they can throw you a bone instead. This was one of those times, the first in a series. At least I thought this had come from them. I should have known better.

"Now I've seen everything, outboards on a Viking! Hey Baloney, you aboard?"

I had heard that voice before, but I didn't connect the dots until I looked over the side and recognized the guy who was now leaning over and petting Thor. Jimbo Morris was the big, burly, bearded owner and captain of the *Can Do*, an older 46 foot Bertram from Deltaville, over on the western shore. We had run into him when Murph and Lindsay bought their houseboat and a bunch of us had gone over there to tow it back. He and Baloney had been radio pals out on the Chesapeake beforehand but hadn't met in person until then. They had been thick as thieves out on the bay ever since, sharing fishing info.

"Jimbo! Glad you could make it." Baloney motioned him to climb on up.

As he swung a leg over into the cockpit Jimbo said, "No way I was going to miss this. Word has gotten around about this rig, and I had to see for myself. It was worth the drive over on my only down day. I've been running back to back charters, so it was good to get off the boat and over to ESVA to relax for a change."

Bill introduced Jimbo to Carrington and Smitty, then took him on a tour of the cabin. I saw Carrington and Smitty glance at each other, then look over at me.

"Those two guys have some good chemistry together, and the fact they're pals for real might work well if that comes across on camera. What do you think, Marlin, is he a good candidate?" Carrington asked.

I liked the idea, even though I'd only spent a little over an hour with Jimbo at dinner one night. But during that time he seemed as genuine as they come. I knew from his reputation that he was a great fisherman, and his older Bertram was still a good offshore boat.

I nodded. I intended to defer to Carrington's expertise if I had any doubts. Granted, I knew fishing and fishermen and was in charge of the funds and the business side of things, but as I said, what I knew about television you could put in a thimble. That part was all in Smitty and Tex's wheelhouse.

When the two came back out to the cockpit I looked at Bill, and nodded toward Jimbo, cocking my head to the side a bit as if to ask a silent question. That's when I suddenly realized the Fates had nothing to do with this chance meeting; Bill had planned the whole thing. While I doubted he had said anything about the show beforehand to Jimbo, now I was sure his showing up here wasn't just by accident. Bill's sly smile gave that one away as he nodded.

Carrington explained to a stunned Jimbo what was going on and asked him if he would be interested in being in the show. Jimbo took his time before answering, starting with a few questions, the first of which was about the pay rate. He paused again, apparently still thinking it over. I liked the fact that he was careful, cautious and deliberate.

"Yes, I'd like to be on your show. To tell you the truth, the first four months of the year can normally be pretty sparse, and now that they're talking about closing the rockfish season that will wipe out my fall, too. I was looking at breaking even this year at best. This'll save my bacon boys, thanks."

Yep, Baloney had planned this alright; he had to have known that Jimbo was in for a rough time with the fishery closed, just like he had been. I also knew he was guilty because he hadn't spoken up to take credit for Jimbo being picked. But I had to hand it to him, Jimbo was as great a choice as Bill was a true friend.

I was relatively certain that Hard Rock, a.k.a. Kim Collier, would jump at the chance to be in the show, and that would leave only one more spot to be filled. We would have to work our way down the list.

Smitty seemed distracted, his interest having been taken by the one Williams' deadrise which was tied up next to the travelift. "Sorry guys, but I want to go get a closer look at that deadrise."

"I'm right behind you." It had caught Carrington's attention, too. That's how we all ended up on the floating dock, looking her over just as KT walked up.

"Hey, Marlin, Baloney." KT didn't seem that surprised to have a group standing next to his boat on the dock admiring her. His forty-two foot Pete Jones was a real eyecatcher and he was used to it.

"If it isn't the U-boat commander and crew!" Junior had been a minute behind KT and joined us all on the dock. "Hey, aren't you that guy from the tuna fishing show?"

Baloney again took the lead, introducing the brothers. KT could see that Smitty wanted a closer look, so he invited everyone aboard. If they were impressed before, their admiration only increased when a thousand-plus pounds of people and dog climbing aboard hardly made her rock at all.

KT showed Smitty around inside the cabin. When they came back out, I could see that if Smitty hadn't just bought a new boat a year ago, he might've headed up to Hooper's Island, Maryland, to see a man named Pete about building a new one for him. KT was proud of his rig, and happy to see that a guy like Smitty who knew his boats appreciated the *Honey K*.

"I've seen Smitty like this before; he falls for boats the way some guys fall for women," Carrington sighed as he watched KT lead Smitty around.

"Want to take her for a spin, Smitty?"

"Heck yes, KT! I'd love to see how she runs."

I saw Carrington's eyes roll. "We won't get any more work done until he gets this out of his system, so I guess we're going for a boat ride."

KT backed her out and headed for the cut, turning the wheel over to Smitty. Thanks to a well-insulated engine box over the single Caterpillar diesel, the rest of us could easily chat and be heard in the cockpit. Junior told stories of some of the fish that he and KT had caught together on the *Honey K*, including a seven hundred pound giant bluefin two years ago.

As usual, Baloney became the "grand inquisitor," drawing the most interesting tales out of Junior for the rest of us to hear. Then for the second time in an hour, Carrington gave me a questioning look. I glanced inside the cabin at the helm where Smitty and KT were deep in conversation, then looked back at him and nodded.

The Williams boys were the real deal, born on the James River, and each having that subtle yet distinct "old Virginia" accent. They had been fishing in the Chesapeake since they were old enough to stand up in a boat, and had made thousands of trips out to the canyons since then. I motioned for Junior to follow me and Carrington inside.

Smitty was talking to KT, "Man, this girl is smooth! I love how the spray breaks just aft of the helm at cruise so you get a clear view to the side and ahead."

Carrington looked over at Smitty and butted in, "I bet she would look good on tv, too."

Smitty smiled and asked KT, "What do you think, KT? You boys interested in being on *Tuna Hunters*? We're putting together a new southern fishing team."

KT's eyes widened a bit as he looked over at Junior who quickly nodded. "Heck yes, we're in."

Jimbo had walked in behind us. "Don't y'all want to know what it pays? I sure did!"

"You're in too, Jimbo?"

"Yessir! This'll be good for business outside of tuna season as well."

I quickly told them what the starting pay was, and they were even more excited. As I looked at the three crews that we'd already signed up, I knew this was going to be a winner for us all. I had thought it would take a week or two to pick our southern team, but now with just one more to go, we should be able to make the press release about the location and the cast changes later this week.

I think that Smitty was even happier than I was at that point though. He had a big grin and was putting the *Honey K* through her paces, going hard over to port and back to starboard, and going from slow cruise to wide-open throttle. You can tell when someone was born to be a boatman. Like a football player who always wants the ball, a true captain always wants the helm, and that was Smitty. I saw his smile fade as he turned to KT and offered to swap places for the ride back in.

"Tired of her already? I think I can trust you not to hit the dock, Smitty."

The grin was back as Smitty turned us toward Carlton's cut, idling down at the mouth to give the big diesel engine's turbo time to cool down before we shut it down. After sliding up alongside the dock and tying up, Smitty reluctantly relinquished the helm. He looked longingly at the deadrise as we started back up the ramp toward the slab. Before splitting up we all agreed to meet back over at the MAFF offices after lunch, to go through all the paperwork relating to their roles in the show. While I had been nervous about getting involved in *Tuna Hunters* at first, I was now more excited than ever. It was starting to take on a life of its own, and I had some very good people involved in it.

*****

"You hear anything from *Tuna Hunters* yet about them new permits?" Captain Clint Bonner was in a meeting with Jim Hendricks, the new mayor of the previous location of the show. Hendricks was a young hotshot with the right family connections that had gotten the twenty-six-year-old this political position, which was his very first in what he expected would be a long string of them. He was certain that he'd already be governor by the time he was in his early thirties.

"No, but it's not like they have anywhere else they can go. We've got the best setup for them right here and they know it. So, just relax, Bonner. It'll happen." He hated the way that Bonner looked at him as if he didn't know what he was doing. He was the one who was the head of the town, not some middle-aged washed up boat captain like Bonner, and he wasn't going to put up with him acting like he lacked confidence in his political abilities.

"Yeah, well, they ain't returning any of my calls, and I still ain't seen a contract yet for next year. I figure they ain't gonna come across with one 'till you give 'em those permits. Just give 'em what they want, and let's nail this all down. It's not like everybody around here ain't makin' enough dough off them already."

Hendricks looked disgusted, "Don't tell me how to run this town, and I won't tell you how to run a boat. I know they'll cave in and pay the new fees or I wouldn't have raised them, so don't worry about it. And speaking of nailing down something, I hear you can't even 'seal the deal' with that widow on the production team. Why don't you just worry about getting laid and leave the business dealings to me."

Hendricks hadn't known that the older man could move so fast. Bonner's hand shot across the desk and grabbed Hendricks' tie, yanking him back across until their faces were just inches apart.

"You leave Tracy out of this you little bastard! You so much as mention her name again, and I'll gut you and turn you into bait strips like a damn bonito. Just give them their damn permits so's we can get back to work this season. You screw this up, me'n the boys'll screw you up, you got me?" Bonner shoved Hendricks back, sending him crashing into the arm of his desk chair and causing him to fall to the floor. Then he turned and stormed out, slamming the door behind him.

Hendricks got up shakily, angry that no one had come to check on him since without a doubt they had to have heard the commotion. As he settled back into his chair he swore a silent oath to make Bonner pay for this. Nobody pushes Jim Hendricks around and gets away with it. Well, at least not many of them.

Chapter 7

It turned out that the Kembe II only had a half-day charter scheduled, so we were able to get together with Hard Rock and Gaffer midafternoon, well before the Beer Thirty Bunch met. As I figured, Carrington and Smitty thought they'd be great. When we offered them a spot in the show they jumped at the chance, looking forward to the extra money and the free advertising.

Carrington, Smitty and I headed over to the relative quiet of the upper deck of *Tied Knot.* I had seen several contractor's trucks parked over in front of our office along with a truck piled with construction materials, and I knew that the walls were already being installed. Kari doesn't let any grass grow under her feet, and neither does her cousin; a new black Sprinter was also parked over there.

After we all settled into some deck chairs Carrington said, "I'm going to catch a commercial flight up to Boston tomorrow. Word is going to get out quickly about all the changes, and I want to bring the crews all up to date in person. Plus, we're going to need to put together a schedule for getting equipment moved down here. At the rate Kari seems to be moving, that new space will be ready in a week or so." He had seen the trucks too. "And, we'll need to bring in a mobile production trailer and equipment storage trailer, so I'll arrange for all that, too."

I hadn't realized that the office space wasn't going to be large enough, it seemed more than adequate for all the folks I met up there. "Sounds like you do a lot more than I thought as the producer."

Carrington nodded. "This isn't your 'normal' reality show that's filmed on a set with standard lighting and audio control. As you know, there's only so much room on a fishing boat, and we quickly learned that we had to adapt to that environment rather than the reverse. It also meant that responsibilities were divided up differently. We have a big post-production crew during the season, more than double what we have now. But we can only put a single cinematographer on each boat without being in the way. So that means they have to operate the camera, handle any audio glitches, and also act as a director. At least as much of a director as the fishing crews are willing to put up with."

Smitty laughed, and I understood why. Anybody who got in the way between a fishing crew and a three to fifteen thousand dollar tuna would likely find themselves swimming.

"I'm asking each of them to do more than they would normally be required to on a land-based show. So, I need to do more myself if I want to keep getting the most out of them," Carrington said.

Not only did I understand that, I respected the heck out of him for it. The more time I spent with him, the more I found I really liked this guy.

Smitty said, "I think I'll hang around down here for a day or so. The new fishing crews will need answers about what to expect about being in the show as they think up questions. Plus, I can help get them in touch with the tackle reps so they can start arranging for some new gear and sponsorships."

"Great idea, Smitty," I said, "then why don't you plan on driving back up in the van with Thor when you go back. I'm sure it'll come in handy up there to bring down any advance personnel and equipment."

"That's a great idea, I'm going to send a couple of people down probably this weekend. We'll want to get some video of the new boats and crews to put together a promo for the upcoming season. The sooner we get that done, the better," Carrington said.

I reminded him, "You can get three out of the four. Remember that Baloney's rig won't be ready until the fall."

"We're going to start with Baloney and *My Mahi*, Marlin, that's a great part of the story. We'll show everyone pitching in to help him get going, friends on land but competitors out on the water. And I want to get some video with the holes still in the boat. Like Skipper from Gilligan's Island putting the *SS Minnow* back together."

"Kinda like *who* doin' *what*, Tex?" Baloney had come up the outside stairs and now looked like he was about to bite through his unlit cigar.

"I meant that in a good way, Bill. Everybody loves an underdog, and the audience will love seeing you bring that boat back from the dead."

"Yeah they might, but you need to be careful about using nicknames like that. They've got a way of sticking to people and boats around here."

I had to stifle a laugh since Baloney was of course the biggest cause of this. But watching his cigar rapidly switching sides in his mouth, I knew he was still aggravated, and "poking the bear" was not a good idea right now. Still, I was going to file the Skipper and Minnow comments away for future reference, just in case. Meanwhile, I needed to diffuse this situation.

"Aren't you back kind of early, Baloney?"

He looked over at me as he settled into a chair. "Hit a stoppin' point for the day, and I'm bushed already. Got the engines and generator all cut loose and ready to come out of the Hatteras, and a flatbed coming first thing in the morning to haul 'em over to the mechanic's shop to get checked over and repainted. Next week I'm gonna have to cut out the aft bulkhead on the Viking to pull her engines, and that'll take a full day or more. Meantime, how about a beer there Shaker?"

Meaning, "How about getting up and handing me a beer." So I did, because it was easy to see my friend was exhausted. I knew he had been working hard in some tight spaces on that gutted Hatteras.

"Don't expect this kind of 'star treatment' from now on, Baloney."

He grunted, followed up by a chuckle, "The only 'star treatment' I want is that per episode paycheck, Shaker. But thanks for the beer."

Smitty said, "I think you've got a few surprises coming up, Bill. Your story, especially the part about bringing *My Mahi* back up and running, is going to make you more popular than you might think. People will start recognizing you in places that'll come as a surprise. Sometimes it's a good thing, and other times it can be a pain in the ass. Though you probably won't ever have to buy yourself another beer."

"Then my life isn't gonna change all that much. Everybody knows me around here, and I don't pay for many beers now." Baloney leaned back in the chair and closed his eyes after taking a long pull on his latest free brew.

Smitty shrugged as he looked over at Carrington who shook his head gently, both silently thinking the same thing; "Don't say we didn't try to tell you."

Carrington turned to me, "Now that we have a full cast, we need to contact our cable network and bring them up to date. Lorne handled all the front office business with them and I guess you will now, Marlin, at least as far as pricing and contracts. But I have a great relationship with them from the production side of things. So, if we can call them together, that would be good. Then we'll need to get out a press release about the new location and cast as soon as possible. Also, I'll get that cinematographer and an assistant down here asap so that we can get some 'B roll' as well as video for the promo. We're about to get busy, and this is only the pre-production stage."

*****

A few days later down in Carolina...

Jim Hendricks' door burst open as a very angry Clint Bonner and a dozen and a half fishermen and local business owners flooded into his office. Bonner got to him first, getting in a few surprise punches to his face before being pulled back by his friends.

"You dumb sumbitch! I tol' you to give that production company what they wanted so's we could get our new contracts. We all just got emails tellin' us that they couldn' make a deal with the town down here so now they're gonna go in 'a new direction.' Wish'n us well in our future. *What* future?"

Hendricks stood up and was backing away after grabbing a tissue from his desk. He put pressure on his nose that was now bleeding badly. "It's just a negotiation tactic, Bonner. They just want you all to do exactly what you're doing now to bring pressure on the town and me. Relax, we've got them on the ropes." But he didn't sound as confident as he had during their last encounter.

"You dumbass! They said they're givin' us some notice as a courtesy so's we ain't caught flat footed tomorrow when they do a press release announcin' a new cast an' location. Some place called Mallard Cove up in Virginia." Bonner was about as angry as he could get, and he had a well-earned reputation for violence. A couple of folks in the group with cooler heads still had him by his upper arms, and they were the only thing right now standing between Hendricks and a trip to the emergency room.

The emails and their content were all news to Hendricks, who now looked as stunned as he felt. "I'll get hold of them and smooth this over. Don't worry, I'll fix this."

From back in the crowd one of the business owners yelled, "You'd better! Or even your daddy won't be able to fix your next election!"

"Hey, break it up! Y'all go on and get the hell outta here before I throw all your asses in jail!" The sheriff just happened to stop by the town offices to drop off some paperwork when he saw the commotion. He started grabbing those at the back of the pack and shoving them toward the front entrance. "Go on now, git!"

Still restrained by his friends, Bonner glared at Hendricks. "I'm gonna go fix this myself; all you've done is screw it up. Shoulda known better than to trust a damn politician." He spat on the office floor as the sheriff grabbed him by the back of the collar and dragged him out of Hendricks' office. As Bonner spun around he recognized the lawman and somehow had enough sense not to send the fist that he had just made. The two had a lot of history, and none of it was good.

"Go on, Bonner, get your ass outta here before you do somethin' stupid. The judge wouldn't be happy seein' your face again so soon."

"Yeah, well, I'm goin'. But only 'cause I got business to attend to. And pretty boy in there," he motioned toward Hendricks' office, "had better hope an' pray I can fix what he done screwed up." With that said, he turned on his heel and rushed out of the building's entrance.

*****

The Sprinter had arrived the day before with two occupants and a pile of equipment. Kenny Vallone was the production company's top cinematographer/producer, and Amy Zeller was their best production assistant. They were the only ones in those positions that were kept on the payroll all year long. Both hit the ground running, quickly offloading the van into the new office space as soon as they arrived after their eleven-hour trip. This morning they started their day over at Carlton's boatyard, getting a lot of video of Baloney working on *My Mahi.*

After lunch, it was the Williams brothers' turn to be filmed as they moved both deadrises over from their old marina to Mallard Cove. I had put *Marlinspike* and *Bone Shaker* on B Dock alongside the rest of my "fleet," making room on "charter boat row" for the two new arrivals. Kari made sure that Barry the dockmaster saved the slip between the *Kembe II* and the *Golden Dolphin* for *My Mahi* as he adjusted assigned slips. The *Can Do* now will be spending the winter season on the far side of the *Kembe.* We wanted all these boats not just together but strategically placed on the bulkhead a few feet away from the deck at the *Cove Restaurant.* MAFF wasn't going to be the only recipient of all this publicity. This afternoon the camera crew became a real curiosity for the couple of dozen people eating and drinking up on the deck.

Hard Rock and Gaffer's turn in front of the camera would come later this afternoon when they came back in from a charter. Jimbo and *Can Do* was on the filming schedule for tomorrow out in the Chesapeake off of Deltaville where he was working for the duration of the summer season. We chartered Junior Williams and his classic deadrise as a camera boat for the next couple of days as the *Tuna* crew filmed Jimbo and also shot a lot of "B roll" video of the area's waterfront for our stock inventory.

I was following Kenny and Amy today mostly out of curiosity and not really in any official capacity. In the case of *Tuna Hunters*, the executive producer was more like a chairman of the board; ensuring the money flow and putting the right people in place to create the show. It wasn't a "hands-on" position. I was fortunate that since I knew so little, the late Lorne Gillam had already done all the hard work by picking great people for the most critical jobs, and I could now rely on them. I was a fast learner, but television production was a completely foreign environment to me. There's no way that I would have ever tried to create this show from scratch. Most of the value I saw before buying it was in the organization and expertise of the people that were already in place. But I was determined to learn as much as possible by watching each of them. I wanted to know about every element in the shortest time possible.

Kenny and Amy had just finished up with the Williams brothers when the orange hull of the *Kembe II* appeared out in the marina basin's inlet. Kenny began following the boat with his camera, catching Hard Rock as he spun the *Kembe* around at the head of its slip. At this point Kim turned with his back to the bow, facing aft, using only his gears to maneuver. Kenny was careful not to film any of the charter customers since they of course weren't part of the show, and this promo was specifically about the boats and their crews during tuna season. He concentrated on catching Hard Rock and Gaffer in action. Once the boat was secured, Kenny stopped filming. I was standing next to him but my attention was on Kim as he climbed down from the flying bridge. Then I heard Kenny say, "Oh, crap." I turned to him and saw that he was looking at a big guy coming down the dock, heading straight for us.

"Kenny! Where's this guy named Denton? I wanna talk to him."

Kenny turned to me and very quietly said, "Trouble from Carolina."

"I'm Marlin Denton. What can I do for you?"

"Denton, ya got what ya wanted from the town. Now get us some damn contracts so we can get back to work down south."

"I'm sorry, what are you talking about? And who are you?"

"You don't even know the star of the show you bought? I'm Captain Clint Bonner. I got the town to go back to their old permit price for ya. You kin get Kenny an Amy to pack up now an get their butts back down to

Carolina." He stopped and stood just close enough to invade my comfort zone. His mouthwash wasn't making it. I moved back a half step.

"Sorry, Bonner, but we already have a deal here with Northampton county, and have already signed a new cast."

"Like hell you say! We're your cast, and this show is about Carolina tuna! You can't move it; I won't let you."

He had me by a few inches and twenty-plus pounds. And I'm not much of a fighter, but I wasn't about to be pushed around, especially by this overbearing jerk. "You won't *let* me? Well, you don't have any say about that, and it's already a done deal. Remember, those same tuna come right past Virginia, so you guys must be keeping what we call Carolina runts."

I know, it was a stupid thing to say to a guy that was this big and dense enough to think that he could force his way back onto the show. But he had managed to piss me off in just under two seconds. I expected a retort from him, but I wasn't expecting it to be with a fist, at least not yet. Apparently, Bonner was a man of few words. Suddenly and without warning I found myself flat on the dock, looking up at Bonner getting his butt handed to him by the Williams brothers as well as Fred and Kim. By the time I got back up, he had taken my place on the dock, totally stunned.

"Meet some of our new cast, Bonner. Now get your ass out of here before you find out what the inside of a Virginia jail looks like."

Bonner slowly got to his feet. "This ain't over Denton. You ain't gonna take food out my family's mouth, no way, no how. I got a deal with this company."

"You may have had a deal with the old company, but it died with Lorne Gillam, and your contract expired months before he did. Now get out of here and don't come back, or I'll press charges against you."

Bonner looked around at all of us, "I'll get all your asses for this, just you wait." He walked slowly toward the parking lot, throwing a few backward glances at those of us standing here. I turned back to the group and saw that Kenny was filming.

"Have you had that camera going the whole time?"

He grinned at me. "Yep! Got the whole thing. Might not be bad to keep a copy around, just in case. A little leverage that could get Bonner a nice spot in jail. I was trying to warn you when he came up that he was trouble, but he didn't give me much time. Clint is one hotheaded sucker. I spent my first season on his boat, and that was more than enough for me. He's a good fisherman, but a lousy person."

I rubbed my sore chin, "That's one way to put it. Hey, thanks, you guys. Even if I hadn't been caught off-guard, I doubt I could have handled him."

Gaffer said, "Heck, you were just getting' warmed up Marlin. After you wore his fist out with your chin for a while longer, you coulda taken him real easy." The rest of the guys roared, while Kenny and Amy tried to hide smiles, not yet comfortable enough with me to know that I wouldn't take it badly. I saw some people staring from over on the restaurant deck, and a few had been taking pictures or video with their cell phones. If any recognized Bonner, this was sure to be on the Internet within minutes.

A customer that I'd seen here before stood up and came over to the railing, "Excuse me, but wasn't that Clint Bonner from *Tuna Hunters*?"

Oh, crap. I nodded, "It was."

"Did I hear you correctly saying that the show is moving here?"

There it is. Internet, here we come. "It hasn't been announced yet but yes, it is."

"The crews from up north will be docking here?"

"For a few months. And these guys are some of the new cast."

"This is great! It will be fun to get to watch their boats come and go. Hey, thanks for the tip!"

I nodded and turned back to my friends. "Okay, here's the deal, we all jump on the *Kembe* and help Gaffer get her washed down fast. Then whatever you guys want to eat and drink over at the beach bar is all on me for y'all saving my butt. You too, Kenny and Amy, when you're finished for the day."

"Just have to put away the equipment and upload today's videos, then I'll be right back." As the production assistant, Amy did the "grunt work." She headed off toward the office lugging all the camera gear.

Kenny pitched in with the rest of us on washing the *Kembe,* a job that was usually the mate's sole responsibility. We all finished in record time and headed over to the *Cove Beach Bar,* pulling a few tables together over next to where the concrete patio ended and the beach began. I spotted Amy coming back and Kari was walking with her.

As they reached us Amy said, "I didn't tell her, Marlin, she already knew."

"I was talking with Mimi on the phone when she saw you get into your fight, so don't blame her either." Kari looked worried as she sat in the chair beside mine. Mimi Carter was Mallard Cove's bar manager.

"First, it wasn't my fight, it was Bonner's. Second, I don't blame anyone for anything, except Bonner of course. That news was going to get around since a few dozen people were watching and filming."

Just then my phone rang. Carrington.

"I should have warned you about Bonner."

I was quickly learning how fast news traveled in this business. "Not that it would've helped any, Tex. He was bound and determined to get his way. Why did you guys even keep him on the cast?"

"Ratings. He was good for a few points every time he got into a brawl with another crew." Carrington

80

sounded tired as he said it. I was willing to bet he's glad Bonner is gone, ratings or not.

"By the way, how did you know about the fight?" I glanced at Kenny and Amy who were both holding their hands out in defensive "wasn't me" gestures.

"It's on the Internet, and we're already fielding calls from the industry news magazines about the move and the new cast. They'll probably have the whole thing up on their websites shortly, and in print tomorrow morning. The new executive producer of a hot cable property gets knocked flat over a former cast member being let go and the show relocating. Actually, it's not a bad thing from a publicity standpoint, Marlin."

"Says the guy who wasn't on the receiving end of that moron."

Carrington laughed loud enough for the others at the table to hear. "No, seriously, money can't buy that kind of coverage. Watch for it on the entertainment news shows tonight. And I'm thinking that the timing of a press release right now announcing the move and cast changes would be perfect. We'll also put out a statement about your scuffle. This is all good stuff."

"If you say so." I liked my privacy and hadn't thought about it being hard to keep because of the show. Now I was not only losing my anonymity by becoming known not only as the guy who saved *Tuna Hunters*, but the one who got knocked flat because of it.

"I'll take care of it. Trust me, this'll be great."

Just as I hung up I heard Baloney walking up, "Hey, I gotta hear about your fight from somebody else? By the way, nice video."

Hard Rock said, "And he's buying food and drinks too, Baloney. He should get his brains scrambled more often. Pull up a chair and get in on this."

I said, "Yeah, it was all staged so that I could get some publicity for the show. See, there's no limit to what I won't do for you guys." I wish they all would just concentrate on the free food and booze. Eye rolls weren't a good look on any of them.

Our server came over to Bill who asked what the most expensive beer was that they carried. When she told him he said, "Good. I'll take two, and an order of wings and fried cheese." Then he grinned at me. Classic Baloney.

*****

The video was great, watching the new guy get leveled by that creep Bonner. A quick first lesson about how there are costs attached to this show. Of course, this lesson wasn't nearly as big as the costs too many of us have already paid. And what more might have to pay if it isn't stopped. Since nobody seems to be able to take the hint up here, maybe they'll catch on when we all get down to Virginia. I'm going to make sure they do before they keep bringing in more people, putting them all in harm's way. It's got to end. How many more are going to die before it does will be up to them. How many are saved is up to me. Greed kills. Stop the greed and nobody else has to die.

Chapter 8

Two weeks later...

"Okay, run the promo." Carrington sounded proud of the piece, and after seeing this final product for the first time, I saw that he had good reason to be. He had made it back down to ESVA in time to oversee the final edits.

Including Kenny and Amy, half a dozen production people sat around the large conference table in our new offices. A large flat screen occupied a big part of the wall at one end which had the video queued up and ready. Dramatic music started as it opened with a wide shot of *My Mahi* up on the hard, the camera then zooming in on the gaping holes in her hull. Those looked even larger now that the edges were ground and faired to accept the huge fiberglass and epoxy patches that it would take to make her seaworthy again. Kenny had deliberately framed the opening shot so that she looked a lot like the *SS Minnow*, and I cringed when I saw it, knowing Baloney was going to go ballistic.

It switched to a shot featuring him cutting out the aft bulkhead with a Sawzall then brandishing it at the camera, looking like a crazed serial killer. The ever-present unlit cigar in the corner of his mouth was a perfect prop. Okay, he might actually like this section after all. Then came a high drone shot from over the marina looking out over Smith Island Inlet toward the Atlantic. In it, Smith Island and the Virginia Inside Passage were on the left, and Fisherman Island and the bridge to VA Beach were to the right. As the drone descended, Mallard Cove and the marina breakwater came more into view with the focus narrowing until we saw charter boat row up close with all the colored hulls tied up side by side. I had to hand it to Bill, he had been right about the whole hull color thing.

Next up was a shot of Jimbo in action, looking aft from *Can Do*'s flybridge. Kenny had been shooting from the water, looking up at Jimbo from a fish's eye view. Then there was *Kembe II* coming into the dock with Hard Rock at the controls, backing her into the slip. Next were the Williams brothers on KT's deadrise. These action shots had all been slowed down for maximum dramatic effect. The closing shot was from a ladder placed behind *My Mahi*'s cockpit and stern, looking forward and slightly down. In the background the first of her old dead engines could be seen hanging up in the air by a come-along winch in the salon, ready to be removed through the space where the bulkhead had once been. This made her interior look like an even worse disaster than it actually was. As the camera pulled back, Bill was now in the foreground of the shot, leaning against the aft covering board. He was holding that wicked-looking Sawzall and saying into the camera, "*Tuna Hunters*. New season, new location, new southern boats and crews. We'll be ready for it, but will you? Don't miss an episode!" The screen went black.

I leaned back in my chair and exhaled loudly. "That's fantastic, except for one thing."

"What?" Carrington sounded concerned.

"There's going to be no living with Baloney now."

The table erupted in laughter. They had all gotten to know Bill in this short amount of time, and he had quickly become a favorite among the new cast. I figured that he might be good, but he came across on video just like he does in real life. He was perfect.

Instead of a usual meeting of the Beer Thirty Bunch, today I asked everybody to meet up at the *Cove Beach Bar*. Jimbo was even driving over for this one. Mimi had the staff set up a long table with "Reserved" signs on it in front of the three tv's that usually were running sports or music videos. Filling the screens was the *Tuna Hunters* logo. Word had gotten out among the bar staff and the regulars that something was up, so by the time the last of our crew arrived, the place was already packed. I kept fending off questions until I finally hit the "Play" button on the remote. As the screens filled with *My Mahi*, somebody in the back of the crowd yelled "Skiiipper!" in a Gilligan-like voice, but they immediately got shushed. Baloney shot me a look that could have killed.

After the promo ended and the screens finally went black, there was a chorus of hoots and a ton of applause. Baloney gave me another look; this one was a lot friendlier. People were coming up to all the cast members offering congratulations and buying them drinks. They were all now well on their way to becoming famous, even if only locally for the time being. The promo would start running nationally in a few months, and that's when it would all hit.

I was interviewed by both of the ESVA local weekly papers about MAFF buying the show and moving it here, but I sicced the Norfolk television crew on Carrington, knowing he'd handle them better than me. Then Kari and I snuck out, leaving our friends to enjoy their big moment. We had a couple of fresh tuna steaks back at *Tied Knot* that had a date with the barbeque grill on the top deck. The boats that we passed on our way down the dock were all empty; the party was getting bigger over at the *Beach Bar*, well on its way to epic proportions.

It felt kind of strange to have our big entertainment deck all to ourselves without anyone else around, but it was also really nice. We both relaxed on a sofa over several glasses of Kari's favorite wine while the sun sank slowly in the west over the tip of the peninsula. Finally, I put the tuna on the grill while Kari tossed a salad. I love this time of year on the Eastern Shore; hot days that cool down quickly after sunset, pelicans cruising overhead throughout the day in search of a meal, and laughing gulls yelling from atop pilings or from the large boulders of the breakwater behind our dock. During dinner, it hit me that this was the first time since I got back from Massachusetts that we both had been able to sit together and alone.

Kari saw the look on my face from across the little café table. "What is it, Marlin?"

"I hope I haven't made a mistake."

"About?" Now she looked worried.

"MAFF buying *Tuna Hunters*. I know it was a great move for the foundation, but I didn't realize how much of my time it would be taking up. Our time."

She looked relieved. "I thought maybe you were talking about us."

"What? No! Not for a second. I just feel bad that I've been so busy lately."

"You aren't the only one, Marlin. This new Lynnhaven project has had me running around like crazy, starting the permit process for the marina, meeting with the planners and architects about the building designs, and schmoozing the city leaders. I'm glad that you're just as busy so that you don't feel like I've abandoned *you*."

Lynnhaven was a huge new project for M&S Marina Partners just across the bridge and is going to be several times larger than the Mallard Cove complex. Right now it is vacant waterfront acreage, but when it's finished it will have condos, apartments, restaurants, shops and a huge marina. So, Kari has her hands full putting it all together.

"Nope, it's just that I realized I've been even busier than I thought. And I guess that's been a good thing, for both of us." My conscience was now clear.

After we cleaned and put away the dinner plates we settled back onto the couch with our wine glasses in hand. I had my arm across her shoulders, again enjoying sitting together quietly while the last bit of twilight faded away.

"Hey, you two up here?"

Against the backlight of the dock's post lamps, we could see Baloney's head emerge from the stairwell.

"Over here, Bill," Kari replied.

Baloney sounded a little apologetic, "Oh, hey, I didn't mean to barge in on you guys."

"It's okay. Grab a beer from the bar refrigerator and join us."

Kari was being a bit more hospitable than I felt right then, since I had been really enjoying our alone time.

"No thanks. Hey, can I talk to you two for a sec? I got something on my mind."

That got my attention. In all the years I've known Bill, he's never turned down a free beer. Ever. Even the cheaper generic brands.

"What's up?" I asked.

He pulled a chair over close to our sofa and talked in a low voice, "I've been thinking. What you're doing for me an' Betty is really special; I can see that now and I want you two to know we really appreciate it. I mean, did you see that crowd in there? People at the bar were fighting over getting my first ever autograph. They wanted me to sign drink napkins like I was somebody important. Betty an' me were asked to dinner by folks we hardly even know."

He paused, there was obviously something he wanted to say, and he didn't quite know how to say it. Kari and I knew better than to push him, so we both stayed silent.

"Shaker, I gotta ask, did helping me and Betty have anything to do with that foundation buyin' this show?"

Talk about a minefield. The last thing I wanted was Baloney thinking I saw him as a charity case. He was a proud man for a lot of good reasons, and I didn't want to take any of those away from him. And I especially didn't want to lose him as a friend.

"Bill, I didn't spend a huge chunk of MAFF money just to help you. That would be going against the foundation's rules, and a ton of nonprofit tax laws. So, I'd have offered you a loan myself before I'd have done that, even though I know you'd never have taken it. But I'd be lying if I told you that you didn't pop into my head when I heard it was for sale, for a couple of reasons. First, Kari and I talked it over and figured you would be great in the show, but second, we knew the show would be great for you, too. We figured it would work for all of us here making a living out of Mallard Cove, so in that way, I was thinking about all of us. And most importantly, I knew it would help MAFF teach people about why it's important to protect even more fisheries. That's been the primary mission of MAFF, and my job is to find ways to get that done. This looked like it was a great tool to get the word out, and if it also helped some of my friends, then it was a win/win."

He was quiet for a minute then said, "I kind of figured that, but I wanted to be sure. Thank you guys, you know what this is gonna do for me and Betty. And Bobby too, since he's gonna be my mate for tuna season. Not a lot of charter business for the *Dolphin* around then, so now I can afford to keep him on through the winter. Payin' for the new boat woulda made that hard this year. And you said I get to choose my own mate, right?"

"Yes, and B2 is a great guy. Plus, he's willing to put up with you!" I wanted to lighten things up a bit. It makes me nervous when Bill gets serious, it just doesn't feel right.

"Yeah, very funny. But I'm serious here, Shaker. Can I pick more than one mate?"

"It's your boat, and our contract is for the captain and the boat. The additional crew is up to you, and you also get to decide how the money is divided between all of you. If you want an additional mate onboard, that's your decision. Though the show has the option of having you change mates if for some reason they don't work well on tv." Bill knew all of this already, so there had to be something more behind it.

Baloney sighed, leaving another pregnant pause while he thought something over. "Okay, I want to add Spud to my crew. I'm gonna tell you kids why, but you both gotta promise to keep it to yourselves."

Kari answered for both of us, "Of course we will, Bill."

She sounded as concerned as I was suddenly feeling. We both liked Timmy, he had been working so hard to build his bait business here. If he had time to join Baloney's crew for tuna season, that wasn't a good sign for the future of his company.

Baloney said, "Spud's bait business has been growing. You two know he hired Andrea to help out at the counter since he has to rig and package all the fresh bait himself, and there weren't enough hours in the day for all that. He's also been shipping out his pre-rigged stuff all over the place by air freight. They're buyin' the heck out of his mackerel in the Bahamas and even Australia now for big marlin fishing."

Bill paused again. I knew he thought highly of Timmy, and so did we. Andrea was the widow of a charter captain who passed away in his mid-fifties last year from cancer. She's also in her mid-fifties, and like so many folks that make their living off the water, the couple didn't have life insurance nor a retirement plan. Word around the docks was that by Timmy hiring Andrea he had helped her keep from losing her home.

"He told me that even though the business is growing, he won't have enough going on to afford more than one of them working the shop through the winter; there's no fresh bait coming in to be processed, and just a little frozen stuff going out. The idea of havin' to lay off Andrea this winter is just killing him. So what the show is gonna bring in for me will be more than enough to keep all three of us going in the slow time before we pick up in the spring. Then Spud doesn't have to lay off Andrea, he keeps his business going, and everybody's happy."

I was so proud of Bill; I didn't know what to say. Fortunately, Kari did.

"Bill, you are such a good friend to everybody around here, so I'm not surprised at all that you want to do this for him. For them. I've watched you do more for others than for yourself. Except when it comes to the last beer."

In the low glow that was now coming from the deck lights, I saw the smile on her face and heard an amused chuckle from Bill's direction.

"Hey, if you wanna catch fish, you gotta help each other by sharing info out on the water. But payin' it forward shouldn't stop when you tie back up at the dock. Beer don't count though."

It was a simple philosophy, but a good one. There was a lot of depth to my friend, even though he tries hard not to show it most of the time.

"Like I said, you're a good friend, Bill."

"Yeah, well thanks, Shaker, but I'm only here for the beer. And I'll take one to go, since it's such a long walk back to the *Dolphin*."

It was a typical Baloney deflection and excuse. His "long walk" back to his boat was just a little over two hundred yards. He grabbed a bottle from the refrigerator, stopping for a second in front of us to finish what he came to say before continuing on his way home.

"I just wanted to clear it with you first, Shaker. And I needed to share that about Spud with both of you. I guess what I wanted was that you two appreciate him as much as I do. But remember kids, not a word about why."

"Right, "dad" not a word." Kari laughed softly.

He chuckled again in response before he finally disappeared back down the stairs. I pulled Kari in a little tighter to me as she rested her head on my shoulder.

"It's funny, he'll claim all the credit for things that everybody knows was only partly his doing, but things this huge that he does himself, he won't say a word about." Kari sounded amused.

I replied, "It's because he puts on that front about being a credit hog so he can get away with doing things in private without everybody else knowing about it. Like I said, he's a really good person."

"You think Spud will see through it?"

"I hope not. And if I know Baloney, there'll be a really good cover story to go with asking Spud to work with him. And maybe we can get some video of Spud prepping baits up at his shop and get him to make stickers for the boats for his business. If he has a promotional agreement with the show and the boats, we can show them on air."

"Bill's not the only one who's a good friend to everybody around here."

I said, "Well, don't spread that around, you'll wreck my 'tough guy' image too, just like Baloney."

She laughed. "I think you did that yourself with Bonner the other day."

"Ouch! You really know how to hurt a guy."

"So did he." She lightly grabbed my chin, "Let's hope we've seen the last of him."

"I made it pretty clear there wasn't anything here for him, so I doubt he'll be back." I may have sounded confident right then, but I wished I felt the same way. However, Bonner was the last thing I wanted to think about, so I turned and kissed her in the low romantic light. He was quickly forgotten. At least for now.

Chapter 9

A couple of weeks later we had Murph and Lindsay over for dinner on our upper deck. Kari and I both felt guilty because we hadn't spent a lot of time with them lately since we had been so busy. They had just returned from a successful ten-day charter themselves, having worked their way from Mallard Cove up to Montauk, New York and back, and were happy to get together.

"Your new sailboat looks great out on the end of B Dock. Nice paint job, and I like the name," Murph commented.

We had the delivery crew bring the Irwin straight down to Carlton's yard where his painters jumped right on her. He knew that we needed to get her in service as soon as possible to catch as much of the season as we could. But we also wanted the hull faired out and painted red to match the rest of our pelican fleet on that dock before she took out her first passenger. Her new name, *Coastal Dreamer*, along with our fleet's pelican logo was painted boldly in white on both sides back aft. Now she matched up with the other two boats and stood out like a big billboard at the "tee" end of the dock.

I was glad they liked it too. "Thanks. Already booking up nicely, especially on the weekends and they have a wedding scheduled onboard next week. That part of the operation fits in well here; the *Cove* is catering all the food."

Lindsay asked, "Are you going to paint your two fishing boats to match?"

I shook my head, "No, since my fishing charters are private like yours are, I'm leaving both of those hulls white, even though each has the pelican logo on their sides too. I haven't had much time to run them lately."

I had throttled back to my most favorite clients. Since I was pulling down a good salary from MAFF and now had a fat brokerage account, my charters weren't as crucial to putting food on the table as they once had been. "Chris has been taking up a lot of slack for me."

I had brought Captain Chris Wagner in originally to run the parasail operation and do some of the winter maintenance on all the boats, but I quickly recognized that he had a lot of management ability. Because of this, I had been giving him more and more responsibility over the fleet, including interviewing and hiring the *Dreamer*'s crew. If I hadn't had him working with me, I'm not sure that I could have seriously looked at buying *Tuna Hunters*. I think he was surprised to have been handed the responsibility of all three boats, but I know he was also really happy with the increase in pay that came along with it.

Kari said, "I wasn't sure at first how Marlin would like being involved with *Tuna Hunters*, especially after we saw how much of his time it's taking up. But it turned out that he has a great feel for it. He and Carrington work so well together, I think it's something that he was born to do."

Lindsay and Murph glanced at each other then Murph said, "We noticed. Your background in writing and fishing made you a natural fit for it, Marlin. Linds and I were talking about this on our trip, and about how the show is going to be such a great tool for MAFF." He looked back over at Lindsay.

She nodded and turned to Kari and me, "Since you made us MAFF board members, we want to point out opportunities when we see them."

Kari said, "You should. It's part of that responsibility we all share."

Lindsay continued, "We've seen what you do, Marlin, and how it all fits in with producing this show. So our question is this, why stop with just *Tuna Hunters*? Why show the mid-Atlantic part of the ocean only at its roughest and meanest? MAFF now has a whole production company that only films for a couple of months, then a lot of very talented people get laid off until the next season. You have to hope that they aren't already busy on other projects when you are back to the point of hiring again, or you have to find replacements and train them. There's a big learning curve in there about filming on the water that takes up time each year."

I had to admit, Lindsay had a really good point.

"You have an idea for another show," I said it as more of a statement than a question. I liked where she was headed so far.

"Murph and I came up with it on the way back down here. You pick different boats and crews and pair them up with a celebrity for the day. Not so they show up and get catered to like we do with our charter clients, but you make them work as part of the crew and have them involved in the preparations. Instead of showing up and hopping on the boat at six a.m., they show up at five along with the rest of us, helping get everything ready. Then everyone onboard takes turns being the anglers that day.

"Show the different target species, the different fisheries both offshore and in the bay, plus both their common and unique challenges. Like the rockfish fishery being closed this year. Maybe even go beyond the boats and show how it hits everyone back onshore, too. From the restaurants to the hotels and even the local farms that those restaurants deal with. The impact of these fisheries extends way beyond the shoreline. All the usual fishing shows stop at the dock, and this part of the story never gets told. Maybe MAFF should be the one to tell it." Lindsay leaned back in her chair; her pitch concluded.

Lindsay and I have had a few differences in the past, but the truth is we have a very close, almost sibling-like relationship, and that's all part of it. Because of this, we can say just about anything to each other. She's not on the MAFF board because she's

Murph's girlfriend; it's because she's damn smart and has very good input. Like this.

"Great idea, Linds. I was thinking that we needed a way to utilize that group, but I hadn't taken it that far yet. You guys have really thought it through. I'll clear it with the rest of the board first thing in the morning. Then I'll call Carrington and get his thoughts on it, though I know he'll be in favor of adding more shows, too."

*****

The next afternoon Carrington gathered the staff together up in Galax, telling them the news about their production company's plan to venture into new fishing based shows. Lorne had talked about it through the years, but he had seemed more content to focus on *Tuna Hunters* and cashing his big checks that came from it. Developing new shows meant risking capital, something he wasn't a big fan of, especially since *Tuna* was such a gravy train. Most new shows don't last through their first season and incur large promotional costs. On the other hand, MAFF had a huge source of capital. With no shareholders to answer to, Marlin and his board had a free hand to explore new show ideas and for many in the room, this was great news. Almost everyone there would have year-round employment, though it would mean most of them would have to relocate along with the company to its new home in ESVA. For several, that would be too high a hurdle; even with their moving expenses covered by the company, uprooting their families was just too much of a cost. But for those that committed to making the move, they knew for certain there would be life beyond *Tuna Hunters*, as well as opportunities in the future that would come with a growing production company. It was an exciting time to be part of it, though once again, not everyone in the room welcomed this news.

Damn it! This is going to derail everything that had already been set in motion. Originally the idea had been that by cutting off the snake's head, meaning Lorne, the whole thing would fall apart. No longer would greed and ego push good honest people to take stupid chances and put others at risk. There had been no way of knowing that Lorne hadn't been the worst person to run the company. Now, this Denton guy not only is going to keep the crews of Tuna Hunters at risk, but the money from that isn't even enough for him. He is going to put even more boats and crews at risk by dangling big money out in front of them, too. Who knows what these new shows will turn out to be, and how much they will increase the danger level for those who work on the water. It is an already dangerous occupation even on the best weather days. No, Denton is even more of a threat than Lorne had been, and now he has to go. Permanently.

Chapter 10

At the next town meeting in Carolina the hall had been packed with very angry merchants and crews, all vowing revenge at the ballot box. Then the following morning an unconscious Jim Hendricks had been found lying in the driveway of his house. He had a broken arm, two cracked ribs, and a concussion. After regaining consciousness he told the sheriff he never saw who attacked him, though the lawman doubted his story. He figured Hendricks was now just too afraid to name Bonner. He also doubted Bonner's story about having gone straight to a late-night poker game on his boat after the meeting, a game that all the players swore lasted until well after dawn when Hendricks had been discovered.

"Here's the deal; we all take our boats up there. We gotta take this fight up to 'em, else we ain't never gonna see another dime from *Tuna Hunters*."

Clint Bonner was addressing his fellow ex-cast members. They had tried everything they knew to get the show to come back, including getting the entire town council to go up and meet with Marlin. But the politicians had come back empty-handed and defeated, realizing that their window of opportunity to bring back the show had long since closed.

"How's that gonna get our tv money back? Even if they film us in the background of a shot, they can just fuzz us out and not pay us," one of the other captains complained.

"Yeah, well, there ain't no show if they can't bring tuna back to the dock now is there? Ain't our fault if their lines run into our props now, is it? An' if they get in our way when we're trollin' they might just lose a little paint. They *stole* our jobs, that money's *ours*. We ain't stealin' boys, we're just takin' back."

Kari walked into the conference room at *Tuna Hunter Productions* where Carrington and I were bouncing new show ideas off each other. We had a tentative outline already for *On Deck*, the show Murph and Lindsay came up with, but we needed even more. Then I saw Kari had a very serious and worried look.

"What's up?" I asked.

"Sorry to interrupt guys, but you need to know that Bonner just called the marina, trying to book slips for three weeks starting just after Thanksgiving. It was three of the Carolina boats from the old *Tuna Hunters*."

"What?" I could see that this rattled Carrington. Like the rest of us, he hoped we had all seen the last of Bonner.

"Our dockmaster Barry Rolle took the call, and he recognized Bonner's as well as the boat names. He told Bonner that we were completely booked through bluefin season. Fortunately, Barry's one quick thinker." Kari was biting her lower lip again.

I said, "I wouldn't lose any sleep over it. They're probably going to try to out fish the Mallard Cove and northern fleets as a ploy to get attention and maybe a future spot on the show. Which we all know there's no way in hell they'll ever see another split second of video. And now that we know they're coming we can keep an eye out for them. Don't worry about it, guys, because I'm certainly not going to."

Okay, I was bending the truth here. In reality, I didn't like the fact that Bonner was coming back, and that he was bringing friends along with him. From the look that Kari gave me, I saw that she didn't either. We would just have to wait and see what their plans were while keeping our guards up.

The next afternoon Bill roped Murph and me into helping pull all the plastic and paper masking off of *My Mahi,* which was now in the paint shed next to the slab. There was so much masking that it looked like it was in a cocoon. The paint crew had sprayed the cockpit yesterday afternoon, and Bill was trying to save money by having the three of us unwrap her rather than paying the yard crew to do it. Of course, he didn't mention the part about us also having to re-mount all the cockpit and toerail hardware too. It must've just slipped his mind. Yeah, right.

"Man, she looks great, Baloney!" I saw the whole cockpit was now Matterhorn White polyurethane with non-skid mixed into the deck paint. The aft bulkhead seam where it had been replaced and patched over had vanished with the help of numerous hours of sanding and fairing. And I had to hand it to Bill, the contrast of the bright white against the light green hull was stunning.

"Yeah, she does. I told 'em to take their time and get the cockpit perfect, especially since this is where most of the filming is gonna be done. Those big bluefin tuna are gonna look great against that white deck. It'll probably make 'em look bigger than they are."

"Not that it matters. You'll probably double their size over the radio anyway," Murph ribbed him.

Baloney replied, "Funny guy. Shame you won't be back in time to see me win this season, Murph. Gonna take the First Annual Mallard Cove Tuna Trophy this February." The perpetual trophy had been Kari's idea. It would stay in a case in the *Cove Restaurant.*

"Oh, darn. I'll still be down in Florida, sweating through the winter and watching the bikinis go by on the dock. You can feel bad for me having to play with schools of sailfish while you guys are enjoying yourselves back here, freezing to death."

"You had better keep your eyes on the fish and not the swimwear dock parade. Remember, Lindsay throws a mean lead sinker when she's mad," I reminded him.

"True. It's not a great idea to tick her off. But she doesn't mind me looking, so long as that's all I do. Old habits and all." Murph had been a major "player" when he lived down in his native Florida. Every day that he was still with Lindsay was a new one-woman endurance record for him. However, I don't think he'll be going back to his old ways; she's a very special lady and those two are meant to be together.

I have to admit, going somewhere warm for the winter sounded great, but I was looking forward to bluefin tuna season and watching those huge fish being brought in. And I know what you're thinking right now; why would someone who is such a big proponent of catch and release be so excited about seeing giant tuna landed instead of released? Because it's a well-regulated fishery, and not a "free for all".

Commercial tuna fishermen are limited to harvesting a certain number of metric tons of the fish, and that number is scientifically adjusted each year to hopefully preserve a sustainable fishery. This came about after the fishery took a tremendous hit via decades of overfishing which kept happening up until a few years ago. Now there are different quotas; one for the seine netters, another for the longline boats, and another for rod and reel fishermen who are restricted to just one fish per boat per day that has to be seventy-three inches or longer. Sometimes the tonnage can be adjusted upwards if the prior year's quota wasn't reached. But no matter what, if enough fish aren't caught by March first, the hook and line fishery here closes until June after the big ones are long gone.

Our western Atlantic tuna travel huge distances, spawning in the Gulf of Mexico every April and May before traveling back up to the waters of New England and Nova Scotia. Some of the school will even split off and end up over in the Mediterranean before most of those come back across the Atlantic. So, it's the responsibility of not just the American fishermen, but all of the world's fishermen to adhere to the quotas. Those are set by an international group whose sole mission is to ensure there will be a good future for this great species.

We have several different tuna species off Virginia, which is why you can find "tuna" on local restaurant menus almost year-round. But giant bluefin are special; very challenging to land and delicious to eat. This is why they bring between twelve and twenty-eight dollars per pound of "dressed weight" at the dock, depending on the quality of the fish. The more fat a tuna contains, and the deeper and more clear the interior color of the meat, the more it can bring in Japan, the biggest and most lucrative market, where prices start at about forty-five dollars per pound and can go insanely higher from there.

"Come on, you two, we need to get her all unwrapped, the cleats bolted and the stainless rubrail screwed back on if she's gonna hit the water tomorrow. I gotta get her over to the slip in front of the carpenter's shop so they can start puttin' in the new cabinets while I do the engine hookups and alignment. I've got a lot of work to get done in a short amount of time, and that ain't gonna happen with you two ratchet jawin' all afternoon." Bill sounded serious, but Murph and I glanced at each other and both rolled our eyes before we got back to focusing on the job at hand. Neither of us minded making time to help Bill, and it wouldn't feel right if he wasn't at least a little bit bossy. You should hear him loudly direct B2 when they leave or come back in to the dock; you'd think it was his first day on the job. The reality is that he has worked for Bill for years, and he can probably do what's needed in his sleep. Still, he gets bigger tips from the charter customers who take pity on him because of it.

"So, did you guys get Bill's Christmas present unwrapped okay?" Kari and I were sitting on the couch later that afternoon, having vodkas on the upper deck of *Tied Knot*. We joked about our Chris Craft feeling like a present when we were removing all the masking paper after she was painted.

"Oh yeah, he's ready to 'splash' tomorrow, then he'll get his mechanical stuff finished in the water while the yard guys install the cabinets. Easier to hand them across from the dock than to carry them all the way over to the slab and have to hoist them up into the boat. He's getting antsy now; he's even more bossy than usual."

"You've got to be talking about Baloney." Murph was coming up the outside stairs, followed by Lindsay.

"You know it. But I can't blame him. It feels like things go so fast when you start to rebuild a boat, but the last third of it seems to take forever," I replied. Kari and I had been at that point twice in the last year with building *Tied Knot* and rebuilding the Chris Craft.

Lindsay came over and sat on my unoccupied side then looked at Murph, "Babe, make me a vodka like theirs, would you?"

I added as I held out my glass, "And a refill for me, 'babe'?"

Murph shot me a dirty look as he took my glass, then made himself at home behind the bar. I have to admit, while I'm still trying to get used to my newfound career in television production, it's nice to have this part of my life with my friends as a constant that I can continue to depend on. Murph came back over and handed Linds and me our glasses before settling into a chair next to the sofa.

"I can die happy now," I said with a sigh. "A knockout brunette snuggled in on one side of me, a stunning blond on the other, and a full glass of vodka. Life doesn't get much better than this."

Kari leaned away and lightly punched my shoulder, "You should have stopped at the brunette part."

"You can be so much like an annoying older brother, Mar." Though Lindsay said it with a smile and she hooked her arm through mine.

It hit me kind of hard this afternoon when Murph talked about their being gone again this winter. I really missed them last season when they went south. At least this year I'd have my hands full with filming the show through most of the time that they'll be gone.

"Oh, it could be better, Marlin," Murph said.

"If you are about to say that instead of a blond it could be a redhead on this side, you'll be sleeping in the guest stateroom," Lindsay replied semi-jokingly. Dawn McAllister, currently Casey Shaw's fiancée but also Murph's ex, is a stunning redhead. She's also a very close friend to Lindsay and Kari.

"Hah! No, what I was going to say was that I could bring the vodka bottle over closer. But now that you mention it..." Murph needled Lindsay.

"Oops, forget I said anything." She took a long sip of her vodka.

Yep, they are going to be missed. "Hey, we're moving ahead with plans for *On Deck*. How would you two like to be the boat and crew for episode one? It's only fair since it was your idea."

"Book us, Marlin! We'll be back here in early March." Murph knew that depending upon the level of success of the show as well as the ranking of the celebrity that goes out with them, this kind of exposure could open new doors for their high-end charter business.

It's funny how one thing leads to another: not just actions but thoughts as well. All of this coming about because I wanted a specific type of sailboat to charter. Then there was Greg stopping by Mallard Cove on his way north. And Lorne Gillam being murdered, leaving

Tuna Hunters up for sale. I wonder if the cops up there have any more leads on his killer? And I wonder if Smitty's boat being sabotaged had anything to do with Gillam's murder? Probably not, since it's two different types of attacks, and Smitty did say that this business draws its share of wackos and stalker types. I really hope though that whoever this dude is he won't follow the show down to here. Of course, that's assuming Gillam's murder was related to the show and not some other business deal or maybe a jilted lover...

"HEY! Earth to Marlin? You're in your own world over there, pal." Murph looked amused.

I realized that all three were looking at me. "What?"

Kari said, "We were saying that after this drink we should walk around to the *Fin and Steak* to have dinner. The temperature is supposed to drop a lot after dark tonight, so it won't be that comfortable up here and I'd rather go out tonight anyway. What were you thinking about?"

I didn't want to put a damper on the evening so I said, "Nothing in particular, just letting my mind wander. *Fin and Steak* sounds great; I'd love having somebody else grill the steaks tonight. We better grab some light wraps before we go over though."

Yeah, I was going to miss these get-togethers when Murph and Linds leave. While I wasn't asking for it right now, I do rely on their input a lot. The video chats we have when they're away just aren't the same. I wish they were going to be here for tuna season and all the filming, especially since Bonner was lurking out there. It's a good feeling, having both of them watch my back. I was going to miss that part even more.

Chapter 11

The next day Kenny set up to film Spud since the season's last mullet schools were passing through, on their way down to Florida and points south.

"These are nice sized marlin and tuna mullet that were netted yesterday morning. I've had 'em in my special brine and ice bath overnight. Makes 'em tougher so they cut cleaner and better when I rig 'em, and it keeps 'em from washing out so fast at higher trolling speeds." Spud was a natural in front of the camera, treating it like he was talking with a new friend. He was in his screened bait shack over on the boat barn side of the store. As usual, he was standing at one of the fiberglass and plywood work stations he had built.

"There's two ways I'm gonna rig these up; the first is a splittail rig for the smaller ones." He quickly gutted a medium-sized mullet, then took his razor-sharp knife and pushed it through the fish next to the dorsal fin about halfway down its body, describing the process in-depth as he went along. "When you're trolling, the two sides of the tail will wiggle together like it's swimmin' at high speed." He held it up, wiggling the head slightly to show how limber the split tail sections were.

"The way we're gonna do these bigger ones is to just remove the guts and the backbone but without making that long cut." Again he described the process in depth during each step. "Now all that's left is to sew up the holes to keep it from washing out. Most guys don't pay that much attention to this part but it's another reason why my baits do so good. I keep my needles as sharp as my knives." He picked up a ten-inch long stainless steel bait needle from a small pile of various length ones on the work station and began rubbing it on a whetstone. "The sharper that point is, the less tear ya get in the skin. I sharpen it on the stone every fish or two. And I use a special and real hard to find clear waxed dental floss to sew with." He quickly sewed up the mullet, stabilizing the hook and closing the head incision with almost the precision of a surgeon.

"This bait right here is a giant bluefin killer!" He held the bait out for the camera as Kenny finished shooting.

"Nice, Spud. Short and to the point," Kenny said.

"I dunno, Kenny, do you think I was too technical? Maybe we should shoot it again."

"No, it was great! I guarantee that most of our viewers never knew there was so much work involved in rigging trolling baits. Trust me, you were perfect." Kenny knew that Spud's self-consciousness would be long gone by the end of the season. He had worked with several crews on their first shoots, and they all worried about the same things. That is, except Bonner, who blamed all of his faulty shots on anyone else in sight. The guy was a real "tool" and Kenny was glad that he was gone.

"How was your shoot with Spud?" I asked Kenny, who had just walked into the conference room.

"Put it this way, Marlin, I'm pretty sure there's going to be a new favorite boat and crew on *Tuna Hunters,* and for the first time it's going to be a southern one: the guys on *My Mahi.* Well, at least two of the three sound like they're from the south. Baloney sounds more like he's from Newark."

I nodded my head, "You should have heard him ten years ago over the radio. And they say that southerners can be tough to understand at times. Ha!"

Tex was also in the room and joined Kenny in laughing at my comment. He said, "Speaking of tough to understand, I'm going to go ahead and put some of our camera crewmen on the other three boats for the next few weeks. They'll need time to adjust to each other. If you've never had someone following you around all day with a camera it can take some getting used to until you're finally comfortable with it. We'll be onboard *My*

Mahi from her first trip out of the boatyard through the last day of tuna season. Those guys are pure gold as far as video content goes."

I said, "You haven't seen anything yet, Tex. When Bill is out fishing he's hilarious. You never know what he's going to say next. I can't even imagine what he's going to be like on a giant bluefin."

"I want to be on his boat, Carrington," Kenny said. "I've developed a rapport with him over in the boatyard, and now I've gotten to know Spud as well. B3 is out fishing on their other boat most of the time, but he's been easy to get along with when he's in at the dock. Though he's the one I'm going to have to coax to get him to talk more on camera."

"Already figured on that being your boat this season, though Paulson is going to scream about us putting someone new with him," Carrington told him.

Troy Paulson was the owner/captain of *MyTunaHunter.com*, the largest and newest boat in the northern fleet. He and his crew always looked more like they had just stepped off a yacht rather than a fishing boat. All wore matching collared shirts with the boat name monogrammed on the left breast which was part of their branding and marketing strategy. However, Troy was best known for being a hotheaded prima-donna. I met him up in Galax, and other than Bonner, he was my least favorite member of the old cast.

"Hi. Am I interrupting?" A nice looking brown-haired woman in her late thirties walked into the room. I recognized her as Tracy Brill, *Tuna Hunter Productions'* finance director. I had also met her up in Galax, and she was now the first of our relocated office staff to arrive.

"Tracy, hi! Not at all. You remember Marlin Denton from up north," Carrington asked.

"Of course. Hello again, Mr. Denton."

I stood up and shook her hand. "It's Marlin, Tracy, and welcome to ESVA. Did you have a good trip?"

"Not bad. I got an early start driving so that I could look things over before dark and set up my computer so I'm ready to go in the morning. Mallard Cove looks nice, I can see why you want to shoot the show here."

Carrington had given me the backstory on Tracy. Her husband and son had been lost off of Carolina two seasons ago, on a day that they should have stayed at the dock. They were the only boat to go out on that late-season day, totally driven to win as well as avoid the wrath of Lorne for not going out. But they were less than a thousand dollars off the lead, and one more fish would have put them over the top. They knowingly went out into the worst nor'easter of the season, losing the boat in huge seas and taking a cameraman to his death along with them. It was their loss that kept Lorne from reprimanding the other crews for staying home.

Despite the tragedy, Tracy stayed on the show's production staff, even with the bad memories attached to it. But decent-paying jobs aren't easy to come by in Galax, and her husband had left them with a lot of debt, and not much choice. Still, Carrington hadn't been sure that she would make the move to ESVA but was pleased when she decided that she would. He figured the change of scenery should do her some good, and at least she wouldn't have to go down to Carolina again.

"We like our little corner of the world and hope that you will as well. I guess that Tex told you that we should be even busier this year, developing more shows."

She looked confused. "Tex?"

Carrington held up his hand, "Me. It's a Baloney thing; he's part of the learning curve down here. But you'll get used to him pretty quickly."

"Please tell me he's not another Bonner. I couldn't get that guy to take a hint and get lost."

"Not even close, and he's happily married, so you don't have anything to worry about from Bill. He's kind of an acquired taste, but you'll like him," Carrington explained.

"Baloney and Bill? Tex? Does everyone down here have two names? Is this some kind of a southern thing?" Tracy's brow furrowed slightly.

I couldn't help but smile. "No. Like Tex said, it's a Baloney thing. You'll understand after you meet him. He was the one with the Sawzall in the promo."

"That explains a lot, Marlin. For a minute I thought we had gone into making horror shows when I saw him with that thing."

I like Tracy. She seems easy going and has a good sense of humor.

"Can one of you point me to my office? I want to start getting settled."

Kenny stood up, "I'll show you Tracy, and help you bring up your computer and stuff."

After they left the room, Carrington closed the door. "I didn't tell you the whole story. As finance director, she went back and forth between Galax and Carolina, overseeing both accounting offices. As soon as she stepped foot in Carolina last year, Bonner was after her. The guy is about as dense as a brick and couldn't or wouldn't take a hint. Lorne had to threaten to drop him from the show before he would back off. It's part of why he was considered a suspect in the murder, though he was quickly ruled out. He had been busy at the time, running back to back charters for a month in Carolina before the explosion. And that bomb was way too sophisticated for Bonner to have figured out how to build.

"He's still got a 'thing' for Tracy, though any female is fair game to him. The two things he loves most are chasing women and fighting, though you already know about that last part. Tracy seemed like a challenge to him I guess. He didn't get the part about being a widow that was still grieving over her husband and son.

109

The guy lives in his own little world with his own rules and thinks everyone else should as well."

I scowled at him, "Yeah, thanks for the advance notice about the whole fighting part, pal. I never saw that fist coming, mostly because I didn't know to watch for it."

"Again, sorry about that, Marlin," he said sheepishly.

"Well, Bonner is just water past the stern, and we've got a good crew now. Or is there anyone else on the northern crews that I should watch out for, too?" I faked glaring at him.

He shook his head. "You've met them all up in Galax, and you saw there aren't any violent ones. Like I said before, Troy and his mate Brian are prima-donnas. Troy's a harmless loudmouth and so is Brian. Both talk tough but won't back it up. Mack James on the *Tuna Tango* is an egotistical kid who's another arrogant, self-centered loudmouth, and his sister Angie who's his mate is very nice but kind of dull. Peter Newman on *Vulture* is an old school type of fisherman, and his daughter Brittany who is his mate is almost as tough as him. She was dating Tracy's boy when his boat went down and she took his loss really hard. We all did. She and Tracy now have some kind of bond over both of them having lost a young man they both loved. Frankly, one day I thought Brit was going to end up in a fight with Bonner, trying to protect Tracy when he acted up around her. Then Lorne stepped in and Bonner behaved a little better after that. And of course you've met Smitty and his mate Gary Saunders from the *Sea Quest*. They don't come any finer than those two."

"It was nice to find out that the Smitty you see on camera is the same guy as when the camera's not around. I'm looking forward to when he gets down here."

Tex said, "You won't have long to wait, he'll be here in two weeks. Since he's the crew liaison, I wanted him here before the rest of the boats start arriving a week later, to let him get more used to things so he's prepared to help them. The rest of the office staff that are making the move will be here by then, too. We'll have to hire some local folks to replace the handful that didn't want to leave Galax, but Tracy and I will take care of that."

I nodded. "You shouldn't have any problem finding good people. Check with Sharon Dee, the Albury's know everybody on this part of the Eastern Shore, and I'm sure she can help come up with good candidates."

I was excited to hear that Smitty would be back sooner rather than later. He fits in well with our crowd, and I hope that he sticks around a while after tuna season closes.

Chapter 12
Two Weeks Later...

The Beer Thirty Bunch meeting had just broken up and Kari and I were headed back to our floating home. As we started down the dock, I spotted a boat coming through the breakwater and recognized her as the *Sea Quest*. We walked over to the slips on B Dock that Kari had reserved for the *Tuna Hunter's* northern fleet. Smitty was backing in as we got there and we caught the docklines from his mate, Gary Saunders. Thor jumped onto the dock, going first over to Kari to be petted before coming over to me and leaning against my legs for the same treatment. While I rubbed his huge coconut sized head, his thick tail wagged rapidly in recognition and appreciation.

"He doesn't take to everybody like he has to you two," Smitty remarked after he had shut down the engine and come out onto the cockpit deck.

Kari said, "I missed him. I got used to having him around in just the short amount of time you two were here."

"Great to have you back Smitty," I said. "And good to see you again, Gary." I had met Gary up north, and now introduced him to Kari.

"I've been telling Gary about how Mallard Cove was a huge step up from where we were based out of Carolina."

Gary remarked, "And you weren't kidding, Smitty. The marina is nice, and I love that it's a straight shot out to the ocean. No bridges or sandbars to tangle with like that nightmare down south."

In Carolina, the current races under a bridge which you have to clear by navigating a narrow channel between its concrete pile caps. Early one morning in heavy fog and after getting swung by the current, Peter

Newman had slammed into one of those caps, causing some major cosmetic damage to *Vulture's* gelcoat.

And yet the bridge wasn't even the biggest obstacle down there. A nasty, rapidly shifting sandbar lay just beyond the span. The channel leading out to the ocean in the pre-dawn morning wasn't necessarily going to be in its same location on your way back in after dark. This is exactly where Tracy's husband's boat and its crew met their end. The boat broached after hitting a big wave in the dark, one that broke over the shallow bar after the channel had once again shifted overnight. It capsized when an even larger wave hit the hull broadside. The Coast Guard report said that the cabin door had jammed when they rolled, trapping all three men inside where they drowned as it sunk.

So, having the protection of both Smith and Fisherman Islands, as well as the safety of the well-marked and deep channel was a huge plus, especially in rough weather. The channel marker pilings are easily spotted by radar even in the dark and also in inclement weather. The only way to find the bar channel in Carolina was by sight, watching for breaking waves, an almost impossible task after dark.

The four of us wrestled *Sea Quest's* two huge dock boxes out of her cockpit and up onto the dock behind the transom, along with a small bait freezer.

"Great! Now we're all set, thanks for the help."

I said, "No problem, Smitty, glad to help. And, we're going to cook up some burgers over on *Tied Knot* if you guys are up for it."

Smitty quickly accepted for them, glad to not have to deal with dinner after a long day on the water. All five of us went over to *Tied Knot,* with Thor leading the way, remembering exactly where to go since he's one very smart dog. But first we stopped at the back of the *Golden Dolphin* so Smitty could say hi to Bill and Betty. Smitty had a mischievous look on his face as he yelled out from the dock in a Gilligan like voice: "Hey Skiperrrrr!"

A scowling Baloney emerged from the cabin. "I shoulda known it was you. When didya get in?"

"Just now. I couldn't wait to come over and stir the pot since we're going to be fishing against each other," Smitty said with a grin.

"Yeah, but that doesn't start for a couple a weeks. Meanwhile, it's a good thing you're around. You can help me get *My Mahi* buttoned up and over here."

"I might be able to put in a few hours, so long as you're buying the beer."

"Dream on, big boy. It's strictly BYOB, and some for me, too."

Smitty rolled his eyes. "You don't want much, do you?"

"Hey, you want to know where the fish are or not? I can hook ya up...or not."

"I missed you, Baloney. Why, I have no idea. But I guess part of it was about looking forward to out-fishing your butt this year. Until then though, I'll help you when I can."

"Welcome back, Smitty. I'll see ya at the yard in the morning. She's in the water now, in front of the woodshop."

"I need to see if they can haul *Quest* tomorrow anyway, my cutlass bearing is going."

"I'll make sure they take care of ya. I've got a lot of pull over there ya know." Bill puffed out his chest like a strutting peacock.

"Thanks, Baloney. I'll see you over there in the morning."

We resumed our walk over to *Tied Knot*. On the way I told Smitty, "You know Baloney's likely to tell Carlton to have his guys stall a bit so that you have more time to work on his boat as free labor, right?"

He looked surprised. "I hadn't thought of that. But now that you mention it, I wouldn't put it past him."

I laughed. "Don't! Because I can guarantee that he'll do it. I'll go with you and call Carlton on the ride over so that doesn't end up happening. Then again, some video of you and Gary helping Bill might not be bad to have. Maybe some of *Sea Quest* on her way over, too."

Drones can be so annoying since they have such a high pitched whine, but in certain applications, the noise was well worth it. The next morning Kenny shot some cool aerial video of *Sea Quest* with the production company's drone. We rode up the Virginia Inside Passage, out into Magothy Bay, and a few miles later we finally turned west into the boatyard's channel that cuts back through the marsh. This all made for a spectacular backdrop in the video. Carlton's guys were waiting for us with the Travelift's slings already lowered into the water, ready to lift us out.

We hand walked *Quest* into the slip using her docklines instead of the engine to avoid drawing one of the huge nylon lifting slings up into our prop. That would have had some really nasty results for the running gear. They raised us until the bow's deck was even with the slab then moved us forward to the seawall so that we could very easily step off. Then they resumed raising *Quest* and moving her farther in and away from the edge of seawall. The crew's foreman told Smitty that they would leave us in the slings and not "block" us, meaning she wouldn't be set down on the hard. It would make things that much faster and easier for the mechanics since the hull would be higher up in the air giving them better access than if she were blocked.

If you've never looked closely at a boat's running gear out of the water, the monel shaft extends through the bottom of the hull at a steep angle. It then passes through a strut near the transom which is bolted to the hull's bottom. The strut is a big brass skeg which stabilizes the shaft just forward of the propeller. It has a brass sleeve which is pressed into it, and that sleeve is lined with rubber which is cast in place. The sleeve is called a cutlass bearing, and the shaft passes through the rubber in a tight fit, cooled and lubricated by the water around it. Eventually though the rubber will start to wear out, and the shaft will start vibrating slightly side to side or up and down. This can create noise which will travel long distances underwater and scare fish away from the boat.

A good captain is in tune with all of the normal noises and the "feel" of his or her boat. Catching the cutlass bearing wearing out early means you get it before it goes all the way through the rubber and becomes metal to metal contact, which is never a good nor inexpensive thing as the shaft starts to wear. Fortunately, *Quest's* cutlass bearing hadn't worn down to the metal yet, though it would only have been a matter of time. Smitty's keen ear had saved him some money, and probably some chances at fish as well.

"They said it'd be just over an hour if things go well, so I guess it's Baloney time." Smitty was in a cheerful mood since the bearing hadn't gone out totally, saving him thousands for a new shaft and the many hours of labor to replace it.

Bill was happy, seeing Kenny and I showing up with Smitty and Gary. That changed when he heard that *Quest* was going to just stay in the slings and be finished in short order. Just as I had figured, he had told Carlton to drag his feet on the repair. But what Baloney hadn't counted on was that while he was a good customer of Carlton's, I was too, as well as being a future cousin by marriage. Here on ESVA, family ties run strong.

"I figured you guys would be here longer, but since there's four of ya, I guess that's about the same

116

thing. I want to get these babies fired up this morning, so I'm priming and flushing fuel lines, and tightening and going over all the hose clamps." Baloney was in the middle of the salon motioning to both engines through the open deck hatches.

Smitty said, "Hey, why don't we stay long enough to help him get them fired up? We can tie up over here after *Quest* is back in the water."

We all agreed, and two hours later a very happy Bill had a boat with two working engines and generator. "That's great you guys, thanks. Now we just need to pull a little more wire."

"The deal was to help you get her cranked, Baloney. You're there, and we're history," I said.

He took his cigar out of his mouth long enough to grin and say, "Yeah, but you can't blame a guy for tryin' now can you."

Smitty's cell rang, and he walked out into the cockpit. He came back in after Bill shut everything down and he looked concerned. "That was Newman. Somebody put water in all three of the boats' fuel tanks last night. He was letting *Vulture* warm up before they headed out this morning when he heard the engine knock, so he shut her down. Brittany saw the water in the filter sump and drained it, but it filled right back up. Same with *Tuna Hunter* and *Tuna Tango*. Nobody else at the dock was hit. First, somebody tries to sink me, now this."

I said, "Gillam was first."

He shook his head saying, "I don't think that's connected, it was way beyond this kind of stuff. This feels more like somebody doesn't want us leaving Galax. Or, doesn't want us to keep fishing. Maybe some environmental extremist group?"

"Maybe. But aren't there other tuna fishermen on the dock? Why wouldn't they have been hit too if that was the reason," I asked.

117

"I don't know. Maybe because we're on television and they don't want tuna promoted as a food source. Or, maybe it was a pal of Bonner's, I just don't know. They're getting a company in that'll drain their tanks and then they can fill back up and flush the systems. But it's expensive, and it'll put their schedule back a day. They aren't happy, and I don't blame 'em. Hopefully whoever did it won't follow them to ESVA."

I hoped this wasn't just wishful thinking on his part.

We all found ourselves back at the boatyard a few times over the next two days, getting *My Mahi* ready for her move over to Mallard Cove. The final runs of wire were pulled, all the cabinets were in place and secured, and she was finally set to go. Carpet still needed to be installed and there was a long list of little details to be worked out, but Bill wanted her over at the marina and I couldn't blame him; he'd have a much shorter commute to work. Plus, *Mahi's* exterior was finished, and she looked spectacular.

Smitty, Kenny and I rode with him to take her to her new slip. Out in Magothy Bay, he took her up to cruise after first lighting up that ever-present cigar. I had never seen a larger nor more proud smile on my friend's face. That was, until he took her up to wide-open throttle. *Mahi* is a nautical racehorse.

Bill looked around at the rest of us that were on the flybridge with him, all of us upwind from that cheap cigar of course. I swear the tears in his eyes weren't just from the cold morning air blowing across the bridge.

"You know guys, I've made a decent living off the *Golden Dolphin* through the years. But she was always the slowest boat in the marina and does like to smoke a bit. I've always dreamed of owning a rig like this. Thanks for all your help and your support, especially you, Marlin. Me and Betty owe you more favors than we can ever repay in a lifetime. By the way, did you bring any beer for when we get her over to the dock?"

We all quickly realized that part of getting his new boat over to Mallard Cove was also about having a larger pool of potential labor conscripts to choose from. You couldn't pass by on the dock without hearing the dreaded, "Hey, you got a second to give me a hand?" Since his new slip was only two boats away from the parking lot, and also since he has the eagle eyes of a good fisherman, he was able to snag a lot of help. Those "seconds" that he talked about usually turned into multiple minutes, and if you had spare time, hours. But nobody minded, we all wanted him to get her finished and ready. And by the time those last three boats from up north arrived, *My Mahi* was standing tall and Bill was as proud as a new father.

Chapter 13

"If the fishing is as good as the marina and the food, this will have been the best move for the show." This was as large a compliment as any that had ever come out of Troy Paulson's mouth.

I had quickly learned that Paulson wasn't happy unless he was unhappy, and he had only arrived yesterday at dusk. The cast and some of the production group were now gathered for a breakfast meeting at the *Cove Restaurant*. It was the first time that all the crews had been together and they were starting to get to know each other. Mostly in a good way, though as you might expect, there were more than a few ego clashes.

Of the group, KT and Junior Williams, as well as Hard Rock and Gaffer, were the most experienced at catching giant bluefin off of ESVA. They had also fished off Carolina over the years too, and I had them give a quick talk about how our fishing tactics differed from farther south. We all knew for the show to be successful, we needed everyone to put fish on the dock. And while these four gave out enough information for everyone to get on the fish, I knew that they wouldn't divulge their best spots nor tactics. But still, it was a good primer.

KT started, "The fishing here is every bit as good as Carolina; but like with all fishing, you need to be in the right place at the right time with the right bait. Every one of those fish that goes through Carolina waters pass through here, too. They just aren't as bunched up here as they are down there. Our fishing is all about skill, not luck."

Paulson snorted, "Then you might as well give me that Calcutta right now."

The northern crews were used to his ego, but I could see that it wasn't sitting well with some of my local friends. I looked over at Carrington, who was smiling. This was exactly the competitive spirit that he wanted to see; conflict was the recipe for successful reality television. I was still learning about all that and wasn't comfortable with it yet.

The Calcutta Paulson was referring to is a forty thousand dollar pot that goes to the highest-earning boat at the season's end. It started a few years back, after the show had become a hit series. Each boat now coughs up five grand in a winner take all bet. Not something that the production company promotes, nor do we allow any mention of it on the show. Some folks think that it played a part in losing that boat in Carolina, and I'm not sure they're wrong. Though everyone wants to be the "high flyer" boat, and that brings even more pressure along with it than that pile of non-reported cash ever could.

"In your dreams, Paulson. Just like it was last year." Mack James and his sister Angie had claimed last year's prize. But it was won on the last day and with the last fish of the season caught by the *Tuna Hunters* fleet. Mack and his sister landed a huge "butterball" tuna that out-earned Paulson by barely a hundred dollars. Despite what would have been a very lucrative season even without the show income, this loss stuck in Paulson's craw.

"You know the difference between us, kid? I'm good, and you got lucky last year. Luck only gets you so far, but skill is in it for the long haul. Don't count on that forty grand again, because it's going to be mine this year," Paulson said.

"Bring your 'A' game, old man. This year is gonna be a repeat of last year. You know what second place is? First place in the loser category. But why am I telling you this, since you know it from experience." Mack had a smug grin that I'm sure Paulson would have liked to wipe off of his face.

Mack's sister Angie chimed in, "You tell him, Mack!"

Remember, I had been warned by Tex upfront that Angie wasn't the brightest bulb on the Christmas tree, though I could see she was fiercely loyal to her brother. I saw Smitty roll his eyes at the exchange. He wasn't the type to volunteer comments unless asked, but I figured I already knew what he would say about both crews.

I stepped in. "Y'all can settle this out on the water. Remember, that has nothing to do with the show. But what does are these *Tuna Hunter* flags that are a new design, so make sure that you attach them in a prominent place up high on your boats this morning. We made custom boat name flags for each of you as well. And for those of you that won't be traveling to be with your families for the holiday, this Thursday we'll be hosting a Thanksgiving meal here in the restaurant. Just let Sharon Dee in my office know so she can add you to the list. That's all I have. Tex?" There were a few chuckles at my use of his nickname.

"No, other than we have some new producer assignments. Here's the list." Carrington passed the sheets out among the captains.

"Whoa! Kenny is supposed to be on my boat. You need to make that change." As predicted, Paulson wasn't happy.

"I carefully matched producer-cinematographers with each crew. Kenny has the most experience with this so he's going with the largest crew of the greenhorn boats." Carrington met Paulson's icy glare with a non-challenging but firm one of his own.

"Who the hell are you callin' a 'greenhorn' there, Tex? I've been fishin' longer than probably everyone here but Jimbo!" For a loud and somewhat tough guy, Baloney could be sensitive about certain things, and his experience as a captain wasn't ever to be questioned by anyone, at the very least he wouldn't let it go unchallenged. The cigar was moving quickly back and forth across his mouth now.

"Bill, I wasn't questioning your fishing experience, I was referring to the fact that your crew aren't yet television show veterans. It's why we need you guys to catch and release fish together as much as you can between now and opening day. Our producers have to get used to your style of fishing very quickly, just as you need to find out what they'll need from you. There's a big learning curve that has to be dealt with fast on both sides, or you'll be knocking each other overboard on opening day."

"Okay, I get that. But no more callin' us 'greenhorns'. Stuff like that has a way of sticking, Tex." He emphasized the "Tex" part, a gentle reminder that the new nickname wouldn't be going away, either.

The crews filed out slowly, heading back to their boats to attach the new flags. I saw Spud chatting with Tracy Brill right before he headed outside. Then Tracy made her way over to where I was sitting and having my second cup of coffee before going over to the office.

"Mind if I sit down, Marlin?"

"Not at all Tracy, would you like some coffee?" When she nodded, I motioned to our server who brought over a cup and topped mine off at the same time.

"That's nice of you to host a Thanksgiving dinner here since so many of us are new to the area, and don't have..."

Tracy had stopped mid-sentence, and I knew that she was thinking of her late husband and son. I quickly said, "I wish that I could take the credit, but it was Kari's idea. Though we both figured that it was the right thing to do since we uprooted so many folks with the office move. How are you liking ESVA so far?"

"It's beautiful, and the people are very nice."

I could almost hear the "but" that should have been coming at the end of that sentence.

"Something wrong, Tracy?" This was the first opportunity that we'd had to sit and talk one-on-one outside of the office. Exchanging ideas was something that I'd been meaning to do with her, and this seemed like as good a time to do it as any. Up until now, I had been more focused on the production side of the business, not the organizational and financial side. Now I wanted to hear any comments or concerns that she might have. However, I wasn't expecting a lot of what was coming, especially this first part.

She sighed heavily. "Spud just asked me out for a drink, but frankly I haven't dated since I lost Jerry, my husband. I'm afraid it might be awkward between us now, working together even though we don't interact on a daily basis. I don't want to lose any new friends here just as I'm putting down roots, and I hope I didn't offend him by turning him down. I know he's a friend of yours and I really don't want to complicate things for you either."

"You're right, I've known Spud for a lot of years so trust me, I know he didn't take it wrong. Don't worry about him; he's an old fashioned guy in a lot of ways, but he's been around the track enough times not to take offense at a turndown. It won't be the last time that happens to him." I couldn't help but smile.

"Thanks, I do hope you're right about him not taking it wrong. But I bet he gets more takers than turn downs, he seems nice."

I nodded, "He's a great guy, and a loyal friend. You guys will be fine, you'll see."

"Good." She hesitated again, obviously something else was still nagging at her.

"You'll find that I'm always up for listening, Tracy. Is something else bugging you?"

"That Calcutta thing has always bothered me. I wish they wouldn't do it, because I know that it played a big part in Jerry and my son Jason going out the morning they died. The whole bragging rights thing is enough pressure all by itself, but when you add in the extra money on top of it, this can make smart people take really stupid risks they normally wouldn't. Can you get them to call it off now that the show has moved? It doesn't have to be a tradition here like it was in Carolina. I tried getting Lorne to do something about it but he refused."

"I understand your objection to it, and I sympathize with you. I'm not a fan of it in this case either for those very reasons. But as you know, it's not something that the show is involved in. It's strictly between the crews, and even if I told them it was banned, knowing most of these guys pretty well, they would still do it on the sly. You know how much machismo plays a part in commercial fishing. Being high flyer means a lot but being able to fan out forty thousand dollars in front of everyone else is huge. So, I'd be wasting my breath to try to stop it.

"The last thing I want is for someone else to get hurt or worse on the show, Tracy. If this was just a three-day tournament I was running, I'd declare a "lay day" during dangerous conditions, and nobody would go out. But this is all about the length of the season and the quota, both of which are totally out of my hands." I really did understand and share her concerns. "Though the safety of the production crew is ultimately my responsibility, and not something that I take lightly."

"I'd like to believe you mean this, Marlin, that it's not all about the money. That was the whole point for Lorne you know. More money for him, no matter what it cost everyone else."

I could hear the extreme bitterness and anger in Tracy's voice, and it caught me off guard. Obviously, she put a big part of the blame for the loss of her family on Gillam, correctly or not. I thought for a minute while I carefully formed my response to her.

"There are a few reasons that I bought the show for MAFF, and yes, one was money." I could see pent up anger flash in her eyes so I quickly added, "Not for me, but for them." I pointed out through the windows in the roll-up doors over toward charter boat row.

She blurted out, "But I'm assuming you'll get paid a percentage of what MAFF makes on the show, even though Gillam used to get it all. That could push you to make some of the same choices he did."

Since Tracy wasn't part of MAFF, she had no idea how the finances worked on that side, she was only familiar with those at *Tuna Hunter Productions.* All of the show profits will go directly to MAFF so she had made a very logical yet incorrect assumption which was made to sound more like an accusation. I guess a lot of people would have taken offense and told her to mind her own business, but I knew that if I did, I'd lose a lot of her respect and wouldn't ever be able to get it back. Frankly, I'd rather swallow a little pride than have her feel like I blew her off. As the show's director of finance, Tracy was a key component in the production company's management team, and she needed to know that I recognized and appreciated that fact.

"You'd be wrong. Not a dime of my compensation from MAFF is tied to the show's success or lack thereof. The primary point in buying the show was to expand MAFF's audience, teaching more people about the importance of protecting all fisheries. And with these new show concepts we're looking into, those will help us do more of the same. Helping by creating a secondary source of income for hard-working fishermen is an important part of this too. Those are the real reasons I bought the show, or rather why MAFF bought it, because it meshes with why the foundation was created."

She stared at me while allowing that to soak in. I think she was still trying to decide whether or not to believe me. I felt like she must've had more than her share of people deceive her in the past, and from what I've now heard from several people, Gillam probably topped that list. The picture I was getting in my head of that man wasn't pretty.

Finally, she said, "I'm sorry, Marlin. This is so different from the way things used to be. Last season Lorne kept driving people to the edge; he had started cutting corners even though the show was more profitable than it had ever been before. It was only going to be a matter of time before what happened to Jerry, Jason, and Dusty happens to someone else. The pressure he was putting on everyone to be out on the water no matter what was enormous."

"So, that's what you meant by him disregarding what it cost everyone else."

She nodded, "Yes. It's why boats started staying out for days at a time when they used to come back in every night, even if they were empty-handed. Crews don't sleep well when they are offshore fishing at night. It's more like cat-napping or half-sleeping, waiting to hear the scream of the reel when you hook up on a tuna in the dark. Do that for a few days and you'll end up like a zombie without getting any real sleep. I don't need to tell you how dangerous that can be out on the water aboard a fishing boat, especially at night. But Lorne didn't want any boats coming back in without fish. He said the show was all about putting fish on the dock, and if these crews didn't want to work harder to catch them, there were dozens of other crews dying to take their places." Her face clouded as she realized how she had phrased that last part.

It suddenly hit me how torturous it must have been for Tracy to stay involved in the show, especially the way that Gillam had run it. It was hard to believe that anyone who had come from a family of fishermen could have had so little regard for the safety of the crews; people that he was ultimately responsible for. Yes, like I told Tracy, that was the way I looked at it. Most of the responsibility for the fishing crews were in each captain's hands. But how much pressure was put on those captains was up to the producer. Tex and I were going to have to change this part of the show's culture; safety was now going to come first, just as it always should have.

"Tracy, I didn't know about that part. Protecting fisheries is important work, but it's not worth compromising anyone's safety, and no tv show ever will be either. I'm glad you told me; we'll make changes wherever we can. The first one being that I'm not going to send any of our production crewmembers out in weather that I wouldn't go out in myself. That starts right now, right here. Without them on board to record any tuna landings, it takes away some of the incentive for those boats to go out. They could still go out, I can't stand in the way of any captains trying to make money for themselves and their crew, but I sure as hell am not going to be the guy that pressures or incentivizes them to take big risks."

She leaned back in her chair, a slight smile appearing right before she said, "Thank you."

I started to understand why she had stayed with the show after it caused the worst day of her life. I realized now that she had made it her unofficial job to watch over the remaining production and fishing crews, doing battle with Gillam and fighting to make things safer for all of them. She didn't want the same thing that happened to her to happen to another mother or wife. I'm glad that she stayed with the show and was willing to share her perspective with me. Lorne might have been willing to cut corners for profit, but I wasn't. Not now, and not ever. I could see that she finally believed I was serious about that.

I wondered how many of the cast and crew knew of everything she had been doing. Probably not many, since she had been very careful to wait until everyone had left before approaching me. Though Carrington had said that she and Brittany Newman had bonded over their shared loss of her son. Come to think of it, with Brittany still on the cast, this might have made her feel even more determined to keep pushing to make things safer. There were a lot of layers to this woman, and I got the feeling that she preferred keeping things compartmentalized and private. But everyone needed a confidant, someone to share things with. Unless that person was back in Galax, I'm willing to bet that it was Brittany Newman.

"Marlin?"

Her voice startled me. "Sorry, Tracy, I was just thinking. You've just laid a lot on me that I hadn't known about. Of course I never met Lorne Gillam, either. Though Carrington never mentioned any of this."

"I can understand why he didn't. It isn't Carrington's style to set parameters, he's more of an artistic person who's into creating the best product possible. Don't blame him, Lorne was the one making the rules, and he made Carrington enforce them. Tex, as you call him, is a very loyal person, both to the show as well as the crews. But Lorne was the boss, so Tex did what he was told. He will be loyal to you as well; just as you know Spud, I know Carrington. Any changes that you make, he'll see that they are carried out."

I nodded in agreement. I was really glad that she decided to lay all of this on me right now so that I could create a safer working environment for both the cast and our crew. If the show was very profitable before Gillam started pushing the crews so hard, it still should be, even without that added pressure. Some captains like taking chances, and I couldn't stop those that do. But I could make damn sure they wouldn't because they were afraid of getting fired from the show if they didn't. As Tracy had pointed out, working on a fishing boat is dangerous enough as it is; there's no need to make it more so for the sake of increased profits. That sure as hell wasn't going to happen on my watch.

We finished our coffees and walked out to the charter dock, heading for the office. We didn't get far before trouble found us. Bonner. He was on the dock taking pictures of the new cast boats with his phone.

Each was easily identifiable now because of their show flags. I saw Baloney and Spud in the cockpit of the *My Mahi*, glaring at him.

Bonner saw us and said loudly to Tracy, "Well, well, well, lookit who you're getting' your claws inta. No wonder you don't wanna look at a hard workin' fisherman again, you're screwin' yer boss man now. Mebbe you were screwin' ol' Lorne back then, too. Sure would explain a lot."

Spud was up and out of the cockpit before Bonner even finished his sentence. "Shut your trap and watch what you say about her, Carolina boy." By that point, he was up in Bonner's face.

"Oh, mebbe I'm wrong. Mebbe she's just makin' the rounds of the dock now as well as the front office, huh?" Bonner stepped back into a fighting stance.

TW and Junior, alerted by the raised voices, came out of the *Honey K*'s cabin and headed toward Bonner but Spud waved them off.

"So, you're screwin' her too?" Bonner barely got that out before Spud started swinging. Bonner blocked both fists then went after Spud with his own.

Like I told Tracy, I've known Spud for years, and I always thought he was "more a lover than a fighter", but he was showing off moves I didn't know he had. Bonner was landing a few punches but not without a big cost as Spud began getting the better of him. They went at it for almost two minutes. Tracy urged me to break it up, which I would have if Bonner had started making headway. Instead, his head was getting in the way. Of Spud's fists. No, I knew the best thing that could happen was for this to play out and for Bonner to get his butt kicked in front of her. Much less chance of him coming back around if he did. Finally, Spud landed one last right cross that laid Bonner out on the concrete floating dock, and he stayed down.

"You watch your damn mouth from now on, Bonner. Tracy's a lady, not one of those dock sluts like you're used to being around. Now get your ass up and outta our marina, and you stay out."

Bonner slowly got to his feet. "This ain't over boy, not by a long shot. I'll be seein' yer ass out on the water." He glared over at Tracy then back at Spud as he started walking toward the parking lot. Spud feigned a lunge at him making him flinch and increase his walking pace. We all watched him climb into a rental car and drive away.

Tracy went up to Spud. "You didn't need to do that."

"Yes, I did. He keeps bringing trouble around here and he's got to learn that he'll get double in return every time."

"I meant you didn't have to do that because he was talking trash about me."

He reached up and winced as he touched a split and bleeding lip. "Yes, I did. But I'd have done it no matter who the lady was. That scumbag isn't going to get away with trashing my friends."

She shook her head slightly, managing a rueful smile at the reference to them being friends. "Well, let's get you cleaned up before you get blood all over Baloney's new paint." She looked over at Bill, "Do you have a first aid kit aboard?"

"Just got a new one for this rig. Got some of that instant glue stuff for those cuts, too."

Baloney went to retrieve the kit as she led Spud back to the boat. With all the action now over, I resumed my walk to the office. Five minutes later Tracy stuck her head in my door.

"You were right; Timmy is old fashioned in some ways."

I smiled. "Not to say I told you so, but I told you so. Also the part about you two being okay. He's a good guy...wait, old fashioned in *some* ways?"

"Yes. It turns out that he doesn't mind if a woman asks *him* out for a drink." Now it was her turn to smile as she turned and headed for her own office.

*****

"What the hell happened to you?" One of Bonner's group asked after he returned. They were staying at a small marina a few miles north of Mallard Cove, where they planned to work out of over the next few weeks.

"I got jumped by a bunch of 'em again. Don' worry, that'll be the last time I let that happen. Here's the boats we need ta follow." He showed them the pictures of all four boats of the new cast, identified by their *Tuna Hunter* flags. They saw the screen on his phone was now shattered, making it hard to see through, but no one was about to bring it up.

"I figure they'll be practicin' the next few days, jus' like they had us do before that first show. We kin practice as well, getting' up close an' cuttin' their lines. I wanna make sure they can't put fish on the dock. We only cut off the fish on these four boats, not the ones on those Yankee's lines 'cause we're gonna be workin' with them again boys, an' we don't need ta piss 'em off. They ain't got a real problem with us, an' I aim ta keep it that way. We make these new boats look bad, and they'll be beggin' us to come back."

Chapter 14

Baloney yelled from up the flying bridge, "Baits are looking good!" This was his first day fishing the new boat and his crew was learning how to set it up properly for bluefin fishing. He and B2 were used to the *Golden Dolphin,* whose fishing cockpit was a fraction of *Mahi*'s size. Everything on board was just as new to them as it was to Spud, who was also "working the pit". Bill could only see the two "short" outrigger baits in *My Mahi*'s wake; both were attached to clips about halfway out on each 'rigger. The "long" outrigger baits strung from the farthest clips were being run way back and were now out of sight, much farther than they would be positioned for normal trolling. But this was Virginia bluefin tuna fishing, and nothing about it is routine. Our trolling speed for bluefin is different as well; five to seven knots as opposed to two or three for regular trolling. The only slightly normal thing about this setup was the two "flatlines" that were run from clips attached in the aft cockpit corners. But both of these baits were heavily weighted and set very deep.

I was up on the flybridge, tagging along with Baloney on this practice day since I was curious to see how *My Mahi* would run and fish. So far, on this almost flat calm day, she was a dream. Not that we had run all that far either; we were still within sight of the tall hotels that line Virginia Beach. This is where our hunting ground would start, about three miles offshore, and today they might run as far as the Chesapeake Light Tower, twelve miles out. Over the past few years, this area has proven to be the most productive bluefin area this time of year, though a few have also been caught near Norfolk Canyon, another fifty-five miles out. Hopefully, they'll be in close again this season, and the boats won't have to make that longer run.

We had the area mostly to ourselves since the commercial season wouldn't open for another week, meaning all tuna have to be released up until opening day. Once the season begins the seventy-three inch limit will kick in, and all the smaller "runts" would be released. The fleet will be hoping for larger fish, ones that after being cleaned would be on the upper end of the two hundred to five hundred pound typical weight range. At around eighteen dollars a pound on average, that makes for anyone's idea of a good day.

Jimbo, KT, and Hard Rock's boats were all within sight, everyone having decided to start the hunt in close. Smitty and *Sea Quest* were on the edge of our tiny fleet as well, probably scoping the fishing grounds and trying some new tactics. There were a few boats in the distance that I couldn't identify, but they looked like they were barely moving. They were probably targeting some other species since as I noted, the tuna that are around here like fast-moving baits.

"Alright boys, let's keep an ear out for 'em. I'll take the first one that gets hooked up. Keep monitorin' this channel an' theirs, too." Bonner and the two other Carolina boats were using an obscure VHF radio channel to communicate with each other via low power, short-range walkie talkies while their more powerful boat radios were tuned to the local fishing channel.

Once a Mallard Cove boat had a fish on, they would broadcast that to make other boats in the area aware of it and give them a wider berth to allow them to maneuver toward their fish. Until that time they were all free to be as close as necessary to get hooked up. Bonner and his cronies were counting on that radio call. They were waiting on the edge of visual range, all idling together.

When tuna are hunting for food, they will often bunch bait up into a ball by working together. They'll circle it as a school, looking similar to the motorcycles in those round "globe of death" cages you see at the fair, then take turns racing through the middle, eating as many fish as possible on each pass. When we're on the hunt for bluefin we watch for that kind of activity. If we're close enough, we can see the commotion happening on the surface. But we also have "air support" on our side. Airborne terns and gulls can spot this feeding orgy happening from much farther distances and they'll flock to the scene hoping to pick up wounded fish or even pieces of baitfish that float to the surface.

Believe it or not, we can often spot these birds with our radar at a good distance if the flock is large enough. Other good signs can be broaching whales and pods of porpoises who also feed on many of the same fish that the tuna do. These two types of mammals are of course very intelligent and in tune with the environment around them, often finding the baitfish before the tuna do. So far this morning there hadn't been any signs of feeding tuna, porpoises, whales, nor birds so Baloney was keeping a keen eye on his fish finder sonar, hoping to spot a lone ranger tuna on the screen. Often these can be larger fish than those found in the feeding schools.

We had been trolling about an hour, with both Baloney and me constantly scanning the horizon all around us for bird activity but without any luck so far. He decided to work our way out toward the Light Tower and we had barely started in that direction when the fish finder alarm indicated something large under us.

"Bobby, watch your rods, we've got..."

Baloney was interrupted by the loud snap of an outrigger pin releasing its line followed by the scream of one of his new 130 pound reels losing that line at several feet per second. Few fish in the ocean had this kind of strength and speed, so we all knew our most likely suspect would be a bluefin.

"Fish on, Cap'n!" Spud yelled as he raced to help B2 reel all the other rods up and clear the cockpit for the upcoming battle. Kenny was right there with them, filming with a handheld Steadicam while several strategically mounted stationary minicams recorded the overall cockpit and flybridge action.

"*My Mahi* is hooked up with a lot of line out. Gimme room!" Baloney said into the VHF's mic.

"Roger, Baloney, *Sea Quest* is veering off. Get 'em, Cap'n." Smitty had paralleled us as we made our turn, and he was now clearing out.

I could see Baloney was itching to start backing *Mahi* toward the tuna who by now had taken out about a quarter of the line on the reel and was showing no signs of slowing down. Bill had already turned with his back to the helm, ready to begin the chase. His hands were now positioned on the single lever throttle/gears on each side of the varnished teak helm pod. The rudders were turned straight, and he wouldn't touch the wheel again until we were back to trolling after we release this fish. Until that point, Bill would use the gears and the throttle to deftly maneuver the boat. On a twin engine sportfisherman, the power of the propellers that were widely offset could easily turn and even pivot the boat within its own length.

Finally, after what seemed like hours but in reality was far less than two minutes, B2 started cranking on the handle of the reel. The 130-pound rod with its curved butt had now been carefully transferred to a rod holder in the middle of the aft covering board; a nylon safety rope was clipped to a special eye on the reel. It would've saved us from completely losing the rod and reel if it slipped from the Bobby's grip during the move, even though it couldn't guarantee us not losing the fish in the process.

"Let's go get 'em, Cap!" B2 signaled that he was ready to take in whatever line Baloney could regain by backing down hard and fast. Bill didn't need any further urging as he got into the throttles, and *My Mahi* instantly responded, creating a surge of water behind her transom.

When we started backing down, there was less than a third of the line remaining on the huge gold anodized reel. B2 was now cranking like his life depended on it. The fish must have sensed the change meant something bad was about to happen and it pulled even harder at the line. With just over sixty feet of depth, the angle of the 150-pound braided line with its one hundred yards of 100-pound monofilament "top shot" still out meant there was a lot of line near the surface. Several minutes went by and despite the water and the air being very cool, B2 was sweating like it was August instead of November, working his tail off to gain more ground on the fish. Kenny was trying to coax more comments out of him as Spud kept encouraging him.

"Atta boy, Bobby. Just keep him coming," Spud reassured him. "You're gaining good, this fight'll be over quick."

B2 was still struggling to keep slack out of the line. He yelled, "Baloney, easy on the throttle, I need to keep this line tighter."

"That's what I need, Bobby. More of that." Kenny thought the comment was for the camera. One glare from B2 told him it wasn't.

"Baloney, watch out, incoming!" Smitty's concerned voice crackled from the VHF's speaker. We had all been concentrating on the line and the fish at the end of it for so long that none of us had seen the older Carolina boat making a beeline for our transom from off our beam. Bonner was pushing his old rig, *Voodoo*, for all she was worth.

"That sumbitch!" Baloney picked up his mic. "Bonner, veer off, I gotta fish on." There was no reply, and no course correction. "*Voodoo*, this is *My Mahi*. Steer clear, I'm hooked up!"

Smitty had already figured out what Bonner was up to, and we watched as *Sea Quest* increased from trolling speed to wide-open throttle in mere seconds. Smitty's baits were still out and now skipped across the surface as he raced to try to intercept and turn Bonner's boat. His mate Gary was now cranking hard on one of the reels to start retrieving their lines.

"Damn it, he's still coming," I said.

"Yeah, heading right for us." Baloney was now furiously puffing cheap cigar smoke as he watched helplessly as Bonner closed the gap between us.

The VHF crackled as Smitty's voice came over it, "Bonner, veer off! You can see they're fighting a fish."

"You just stay the hell out of it, Smitty. I ain't got nothin' against you and the rest of that Yankee fleet. But these boys are gonna learn the hard way that nobody steals jobs away from me an' the rest of the boys from down South. We aim ta make sure they don't land a single damn fish. Not now, and not in season, neither. You just back off an' lemme do what I gotta do."

Smitty's voice sounded like ice as he replied, "That isn't gonna happen, Bonner. You pick a fight with them, and you'll be picking a fight with all of us, too. They didn't 'steal' your jobs; your local government screwed that up for you. Blame them if you want to blame somebody, but don't take it out on these guys; they're just trying to make a living like the rest of us."

The radio went silent, and *Voodoo* kept to her course. Kenny had been recording everything, and now he panned over to the two approaching boats. Originally he had hoped to get some decent "B roll" for fill in and promos, but he had realized this might end up being more than that, depending on what Bonner did. He was locked on the two approaching boats where it soon became obvious that Smitty wouldn't be able to reach Bonner before *Voodoo* got close to *Mahi*. He broke off the pursuit, slowing back to idle speed.

I grabbed the mic, "Bonner, this is Marlin Denton. Smitty is right; these boats and their crews didn't steal your jobs, your local politicians' greed did. You want to put blame somewhere, that's where you need to look."

This time Bonner replied, "*You!* You're even more ta blame. I know you'd a screwed us outta our jobs anyway. Well, I'm a generous kinda guy. I'm willin' to forget about that iff'n you jes hire us back an' move the show back to where it belongs. Hell, you kin even bring them lousy job stealin' Virginians with you, we'll whup both them and the Yankees out on the water. But I'm tellin' you, iff'n you don't move it back to Carolina, there ain't gonna be no show this year, and you're gonna be seein' *this* every day."

Voodoo was now less than fifty yards away, on a course that would take her about ten yards aft of *Mahi's* stern. Baloney was cursing a blue streak and had dropped his cigar in the process. He was yelling loud enough that Bonner heard him from his flybridge when he passed by, parting the fishing line in the process. There was still enough line out at that point so its angle from the rod tip brought it way closer to the surface than Bonner's running gear, which was just over five feet below the water. His propellers went right through the monofilament, which at that point was pulled as tight as a guitar string. The wake from *Voodoo* now rocked *My Mahi* and sent a surge of water over the stern.

"That sonofabitch thinks he's gonna get away with doing that, he's got another thing comin'! I'm not about to stand for this! He pulls this crap again and I'll hole his hull!" Baloney, like many liveaboards and offshore rigs, kept several firearms onboard.

I knew that we needed to do something to stop this, but I didn't want to see things escalate to that point. The seeds of a plan were starting to come together in my mind. However, before I could share it with Baloney, a scream erupted from below in the cockpit. He

139

and I leaned over the aft bridge railing and looked down to where Kenny was doing a wild dance, reaching around to his back with both hands and yanking his shirttail out of his pants. We had just discovered what had happened to Baloney's lost cigar. Kenny picked it up from the deck then glared up at Baloney.

"Oops, sorry there, Kenny. But ya mind passing that back up here? I just lit it."

Kenny's silent response was to hurl the offensive stogie over the transom and into *Mahi's* wake, glare up at Bill then grab his camera and return to filming, all over Baloney's loud protests. But this happened at a good point, if there is ever a good point to have a cigar fall down the back of somebody's shirt. It diffused the situation just long enough for my idea to gel. I asked Kenny to kill the cameras and mics here on the bridge for a few minutes. I needed to have a conversation with Baloney. A very private conversation.

"Bill, apparently this is why those three boats all came up here, and from what Bonner said, it sounds like they plan to keep doing this. They think they can strongarm their way back onto the show by breaking off all our tuna."

"Yeah, well, wait'll they try that again and they'll get some lead below the waterline!" He was still furious, and rightfully so. I figured he would be, which is why I had Kenny kill the mics. I held up my open palms, trying to calm him down so he could hear me out.

I said, "You start shooting and you'll only end up going to jail, which would make the Carolina crews happy. No, what we need to do is cost them some money, just like Bonner wants to do to all of us. We need to play their game, but by our rules." As I outlined my plan, Baloney's scowl turned into a wide grin.

"Think it's still there, Marlin?"

I nodded. "Looked like it had been there a while. We need to go talk to Carlton in person, I don't want anybody overhearing a call to him about it."

"Gotcha." Baloney went to the aft rail, "Nevermind putting out more baits. Kenny, kill the rest of those cameras, wouldya? Then Bobby and Spud, you guys come up here, I gotta tell you something."

After we all huddled up on the flybridge, since we were still in range of the VA Beach cell towers, I called Smitty to tell him why we were leaving. Then I did the same with our southern crews. I asked them to do nothing to dissuade Bonner and his pals from pulling the same stunt again today. We needed them to be overconfident tomorrow morning. Then I climbed down and talked to Kenny, telling him that we were knocking off for the day. He's no dummy and gave me a sideways look.

"I'm guessing this is about what Bonner did, and whatever this is it's also on a 'need to know' basis which is why you didn't want me up on the bridge."

I replied, "Yep, need to know, and you don't want to know. Yet. You'll see soon enough."

Baloney set our course for the Virginia Inside Passage, then up to Magothy Bay and Carlton's boatyard. As we pulled up I saw what we came for still lying on the ground. Carlton had seen us coming in from his office window and had headed to the dock in front of the slab to meet us. Baloney and I jumped off and met him onshore. He looked concerned.

"I heard you were all out fishing that rig. You break something already, Bill?"

"Nothin' like that Carlton. Got a favor to ask. You wanna sell that old hawse line over there?" Baloney indicated a several-hundred-foot length of dark three-inch polypropylene line piled up in the dirt next to the fence.

"That thing? It was floating just offshore when Claude Wright hit it in his deadrise. Stalled his Detroit 6V-71 and bent his prop. We hacked a chunk of it off just getting it out of the running gear. Must've come from an ocean tug. I was going to sell it to a restaurant for decoration, but never got around to it. If you guys need it, you can have it for free. But unless you're pulling a cruise ship, it'll be a ton of overkill. Weighs a lot, too."

I spoke up. "We need it. But we don't want a lot of folks knowing about it." I told him the plan. I could trust him, he's family. Plus, he was ticked off to learn about why we needed it.

"All of my crew are at lunch, so let's drag this thing down to your boat now, before they get back." With Spud and Bobby helping, we made quick work of it. Kenny had offered, but I didn't want any of *Tuna Hunter Productions* employees to have anything to do with this. With the hawser now safely on the deck of the cockpit, we headed back to Mallard Cove, we had rigging to do.

When we reached the almost two-mile inland cut that runs from Skidmore Island down to the marina, Baloney throttled back to idle. This gave Spud and B2 time to put up the cockpit cover, a white canvas cover that hangs from the back of the flybridge deck down to the transom gunwale's covering board. You see these a lot on sportfishing boats with teak decks and varnished bulkheads since they protect them from the sun at the dock yet they leave plenty of room to move around under them in the forward part of the cockpit. Baloney had this one made because he and Betty live aboard. Their slip is in sight of the *Cove's* deck, so it gives them privacy in the summer when there are a lot of people dining outside. It also had side flaps that completely tent the cockpit when they are lowered and snapped to the side of the cabin. This afternoon, we would be able to avoid any prying eyes.

Kenny headed to the office to download the video that had been taken today, and I wasn't surprised to hear Carrington on the dock ten minutes later.

"Hey, is anyone on board?"

I carefully undid the forward edge of the side flap and stuck only my head out, still blocking any view of the cockpit. "Tex, you need to go away."

"Huh? What do you mean, Marlin, and what's that gawd awful smell?"

"I mean that you need to trust me. Nevermind the smell, you'll find out soon enough. Now, get out of here before somebody sees you." I snapped the side flap closed again, leaving one very confused former Texan on the dock. Baloney was using a plumbers torch to heat up a Phillips screwdriver, melting his way through the ends of each of the now twin halves of polypropylene hawser line that we'd cut. Tex had been right, the smell was really awful. Baloney had already used the torch to melt all four ends of the lines to keep them from fraying apart, which was what had caused the majority of the smell. But it would all be worth it if they performed like I hoped. We had just a little more rigging to do.

Chapter 15

After we had headed over to Carlton's yesterday, Jimbo and Hard Rock each hooked up with some nice bluefin. Like us, they were both then cut off by two of Bonner's cronies just as he'd threatened, and just like I wanted. As I said, we needed them to be overconfident. My original plan was to use KT's boat as well as Bill's for today's operation, but Hard Rock and Gaffer insisted on getting revenge since it had cost them a full spool of braided fishing line. I couldn't argue with their thinking; that line wasn't cheap.

This morning our little fleet again consisted of our four southern boats and *Sea Quest*. I had tried like heck to get Smitty to leave it to us, but he insisted on being there in person to see Bonner get what was coming to him. Another argument that I lost, not that I tried too hard to win it.

The five of us headed out early, and just like yesterday the Carolina boats were waiting for us, staying just in our sight as they followed us. Fortunately, that meant they weren't close enough to see exactly what we were up to. We idled down when we were about three and a half miles out, then Hard Rock headed north and Baloney turned south. We wanted the sun in the eyes of the Carolina boats as they approached from the west.

We had all six rods in their holders as usual, but today we didn't put out any bait. Instead, *we* were the bait. B2 had attached a big sea anchor to the only flatline rod we would use. A sea anchor is a big fabric cone-shaped drogue chute designed to keep a boat's bow pointed into the wind while drifting. But instead of being dragged by it, we would be doing the reverse. This was a variation on an old sportfishing gag.

If you ever have a friend that falls asleep in the fighting chair on a slow day, you need to do something to liven things up. Like clipping a weighted five gallon bucket to one of the lines when you are in deep water. Let out half a reel's worth of line or more on silent free spool while the bucket sinks. Set the drag on the reel very light then flip on the clicker while the captain gooses the throttle. It sounds just like a big fish strike with line peeling off. Keeping the boat in gear so the bucket creates drag, it'll take seemingly forever to get all the line back. It also helps to give a little narration during the process to "sell" the whole thing. I admit, I'm guilty of having done it a couple of times myself.

This morning, the sea anchor replaced the weighted bucket because we needed the line to stay up closer to the surface while still bending the heck out of the rod. This was our decoy, and we were going to set the trap next. On the opposite side of the cockpit, Spud started feeding out one of the two hawsers which we had nicknamed our water snakes. The other one was on Hard Rock's *Kembe,* and Gaffer was now dropping it back as well. Each was about a hundred feet long and almost black in color, rendering it invisible in today's light chop, especially with the sun still low on the horizon and in the eyes of boats approaching from the west. Baloney had run 300-pound test monofilament line through those holes he had melted in the snakes. The far end had a large older Kona head lure attached to it. The other had about forty feet of the heavy monofilament with a looped end that Spud now attached to the aft cleat on that corner. The hawser was neutrally buoyant, leaving it dragging just below the surface as Baloney kept us moving forward at two knots.

Baloney picked up his phone, "You set? Okay, here goes."

He hung up the phone and grabbed the mic, "*My Mahi* is hooked up, gimme room boys!" He grinned over at me, and then looked at his radar screen. Thirty seconds later he said, "Here he comes." Bonner was on the move.

"*Kembe* is hooked up, veer off for me, Jimbo."

"Gotcha Kim, I'm giving you room. Catch 'em up!"

Baloney kept watching the screen. "And we have our next contestant! Looks like he'll hit Hard Rock about the same time as Bonner gets here."

I waited until Bonner's boat was a quarter-mile away, then I took the mic. "*Voodoo*, this is *My Mahi*. Bonner, this is Marlin Denton, I'm warning you we have a fish on and so does *Kembe*. You and your guys need to stay clear of our lines and give us room to land our fish or else. No more playing around like yesterday, we're not going to put up with it. Veer off now."

"Yer not gonna put up with it? What're you gonna do, beat my fist up with your face again? You're not gonna land one fish until you hire us an' move the show back, you got that? Until ya do, yer gonna keep losin' tackle."

I replied tersely, "Last warning, Bonner, steer clear of our lines or we're not responsible for what happens."

"Screw you, Denton." The radio went silent except for Hard Rock who issued the same warning to the boat aiming for his lines. He received a similar reply from that Carolina captain.

I looked over at Kenny who had his Steadicam camera with him up on the flybridge, and he gave me a "thumbs up" since he'd gotten the whole conversation on the video. We all turned and faced aft, watching as Bonner's boat approached at about the same distance as he had yesterday. Hopefully, he either wouldn't notice or it wouldn't register with him that we weren't backing down and were still moving forward. I almost held my breath as I watched him bear down on our first line.

The rod with the sea anchor recoiled when the line parted. Less than a second later came a sound like

146

a shot as the 300-pound monofilament line attached to our water snake and our cleat snapped as the hawser was snared by Voodoo's running gear. Bonner saw it a split second before running it over, far too late to be able to react and stop what was about to happen. *Voodoo* had been moving forward at a little over twenty knots when she started winding up the hawser on both propellers. Floating hawsers are one of the biggest dangers in the ocean, right up there with lost metal cargo containers, wood pallets, and logs. Any one of them can wipe out your running gear in a split second, and that's what happened with *Voodoo*. Both of her engines were fitted with reduction gears which multiplied the torque to each shaft, much more than the big diesels that powered them.

We heard his engines start to scream when they no longer had any load attached. The hawser had found the weakest links of the running gear on both sides. The starboard shaft had snapped between the propeller and the strut as both propellers wound up the huge line between them. The thick woven polypropylene line has almost no stretch in such a short distance. Once the starboard prop was gone, the port prop was free to wind up the remaining hawser from both sides like a big tuna reel. Unfortunately, it ran out of space between the shaft and the hull within seconds. The strut had been secured with four huge carriage bolts that passed through the fiberglass coated wooden hull into a thick wood backing plate in the lazarette. But for years *Voodoo* had been run hard as a commercial charter boat. Meaning that Bonner's attention to maintenance was mostly limited to changing engine oil and an annual bottom cleaning each spring. Had he stuck his head through the hatch into the lazarette on occasion he might have discovered the soft wood rot in the bottom. Cracked and chipped paint had allowed water to soak into the wooden hull around and under the backing plate. That part of the lazarette had only been painted once, back when she was built, some thirty years before. It should have been painted many times since then, protecting the wood, and sealing out the water which continually dripped from the port rudder's thru-hull stuffing box.

The torque on the shaft probably would have snapped off this prop as well if the wood around the backing plate hadn't been so soft. Instead, the bottom gave way when the hawser had no more room to wrap around the shaft and had begun pushing on the bottom. The pressure on that strut had been intense. This ripped an almost one-foot hole in the hull when the backing plate was pulled through the weakened bottom, still attached to the strut. The hawser continued to wind around the now wildly flailing monel shaft until it also snapped up near where it passed through the hull into the engine room. The weight of the broken running gear dragged the rest of the hawser down with it to the bottom, almost eighty feet below.

Voodoo's fate was now sealed, though Bonner had yet to fully realize it. He was focused on controlling his two runaway engines that were overrevving. Bonner brought both back to idle and then shifted into neutral as *Voodoo* coasted to a stop a hundred yards from us. His mate had heard the big noise back aft and lifted the port lazarette hatch. What he saw made his blood run cold.

"Clint! We been holed!"

Up on the flybridge Bonner turned and said, "What?"

"We're goin' down, Cap'n! This thing's a foot across! Ain't gonna be no fixin' it. We gotta get offa her!"

From his vantage point on the bridge, Bonner could see the ocean's blue color through the hatch, and quickly realized that what his mate had said was true. Water was rushing into the hull far faster than his bilge pumps could ever begin to pump it out, and there would be no stopping it. At the rate she was already settling, the cockpit scuppers would start adding more water to the problem very quickly. If they went into the fifty-degree water, even with life jackets on, they wouldn't last for more than fifteen minutes before being overcome by hypothermia. He grabbed his mic.

"Billy! Get your ass over here. We been holed, an' she's goin' down fast!"

Suddenly I felt like I had been punched in the gut. I looked over at Baloney, and he looked as shocked as I felt. This wasn't part of the plan; we had intended to disable Bonner, not sink him. He started turning *My Mahi* toward the doomed boat.

The radio squawked, "I cain't, Clint. Somethin's caught in my prop, an' I'm dead in the water." It sounded like Hard Rock and Gaffer had been on target as well.

Baloney picked up his mic, "Hang on Bonner, we'll be there in a minute to take you and your mate off."

"You yankee sumbitch! You holed mah boat! Stay th' hell away from me! Ah'll shoot yer ass if you get near here! Willie, come'n get us!"

"We'll be there'n two minutes, Clint. Hang on, boys," the third Carolina captain replied.

Rule number one on the ocean is that you never leave a boat in peril, even if they refuse assistance and you can't stand the jerk. Baloney knew that, so he still moved over within twenty yards of Bonner's rig. She was now visibly down in the stern, the scuppers nearly a foot under water ("underwater"). Bonner and his mate kept going into the cabin, trying to save as many of their belongings as they could. By the time their friend's boat arrived, the aft gunwale was almost awash. They passed what they could over onto that boat, then climbed aboard as *Voodoo* started to roll to starboard. His friend gunned his engine, moving out from under the path of the port outrigger and tuna tower. Then he moved over to within ten yards of us.

Bonner shook his fist and yelled, "Ah'll get you sumbitches fer this! Ah'll kill all y'all! Nobody sinks me an' gets away with it!"

As bad as I felt about sinking his boat, I'd had more than enough of his mouth. "You sunk yourself you dumbass! We got it all on video, Bonner. You mess with us anymore and we'll send a copy to the Coast Guard who'll yank both you and your other pal's licenses, and your charter days will be over. We'll also send a copy to your insurance company showing how we repeatedly warned you to stay clear of our lines; that we wouldn't be held responsible if you didn't. They see that and there's no way they'll pay your claim. So, I'll sit on that video if you and your pals clear out of Virginia today. But if I see either of your boats around here again, I'll make sure those videos go right out, you got me?"

Bonner shook his fist, "Screw you, Denton! Ah ain't done with you! We ain't even, not by ah long shot. You jus' wait, I'll get yer ass!"

"Fine Bonner, whatever. Maybe we'll wait until your insurance company pays you before we send them that video. That way they can get you for fraud, and you can go to prison on top of it all. That's your choice."

I was interrupted by a loud hissing sound as the glass in *Voodoo's* front hatch blew out. She was down now by the stern, only the bow deck from the wheelhouse forward and the tower's buggy top were still sticking above the water. Air pressure had built up in the sinking cabin and the hatch glass was the weakest point left from where it could escape. We all fell silent as we watched the final minutes before she slipped completely below the surface of the cold Atlantic.

I saw Bonner turn toward us now totally enraged, spewing a string of profanities and again vowing revenge. When he paused I addressed his friend who was running the boat. Kenny was behind me and kept recording.

"Captain take my advice and get Bonner to listen to reason. You're tied up in this now, too."

He replied, "I ain't done nothing to you, Denton. You're the one who fired us all."

"You conspired with Bonner to harass us and cost us valuable fish and tackle. Now you know that if he tries to get his insurance to pay for that boat under false pretenses, you'll be guilty of conspiracy to commit fraud because you knew all about it. Think about that and get him to calm down. Then get the hell out of Virginia or things are gonna get ugly, really fast. You need to call the Coast Guard and make a report about the sinking. I've got friends there; I'll know what gets put in that report, so think about it very hard and be smart when you give them your statement." I turned to Baloney, "Let's go home."

Bill gunned the engines and *My Mahi's* bow rose as her hull began planing across the surface and she picked up speed. Spud and B2 joined us on the bridge for the ride back in.

Kenny now stopped recording and carefully lay his camera down on one of the seats. "Marlin, I wouldn't count on Bonner heading back just yet. He's not that smart, and he's a hotheaded bully. I'd watch your back if I were you."

"Thanks, Kenny. You may be right; in addition to his boat he lost a lot more 'face' back there and that won't sit too well with him. He'll at least have to make his buddies think that he's gotten revenge. But hopefully he'll be smart enough to know I'm not bluffing about the videos."

"But you guys set a trap for him with that hawser line."

I smiled, "One man's hawser line is another man's fishing experiment. Did it or did it not have a lure with a hook attached?"

"Yeah, it did. But it wasn't attached to any rod or reel."

Baloney answered, "What? You never heard of a handline before?" He frowned, "Besides, he had it comin', he called me a Yankee."

"Bill, you sound like a Yankee, and you were raised in New Jersey. He's got a point there," I said.

"No, I'm a *transplant*; there's a difference. I've been here almost half my life, which means I'm almost a native. I'm an honorary southerner, y'all."

That sounded so very wrong, "Y'all" said with a Jersey accent. But I didn't push the point, it could have been worse. He could have said "Youse all."

Late that afternoon I got a call from Carlton. "I've got a Carolina boat over here in the slings with a very familiar-looking hawser. You want your lure back?" I didn't need to see his face; I already knew he was smiling ear to ear.

"I have no idea what you're talking about, Carlton, my lures are all where they should be." I couldn't help but chuckle.

"This guy is lucky. It's a single engine and the hawser wound up between the prop and his strut. Pulled the shaft straight out of the gear coupling, but not past the stuffing box. So, she didn't take on any water or lose the prop and shaft. It could've been a lot worse, but I'll have him back running in an hour or so. And speaking of worse, he said his buddy also ran into something and ended up losing his boat this morning." The pregnant pause that came after this made it more like a statement than a question.

"Do tell. Well, Carlton, you'd think those Carolina boys would have their share of stuff floating down there, too, and they'd know to be more careful. Especially about who they pick fights with."

"Remind me never to make you mad, Marlin. Speaking of which, are you going over to Sam's tomorrow at noon?"

"Oh, right, Thanksgiving. I almost forgot. Yes, we'll be there, and then we have a second dinner over here tomorrow night."

The "there" part of that is Kari's parent's house, and Sam is her dad's name. His house was not somewhere I'm very comfortable being, but as I mentioned earlier, I'd do anything for her. And I had gotten along a little better with her father at our *Tied Knot* launching party, though we hadn't seen each other since.

"I'll see you two over there. Maybe we can sit and have a beer."

"Count on it, Carlton. See you there." I hung up.

Other than Kari, Carlton is my favorite in the Albury family since he has always gone out of his way to try to make me feel comfortable at their family gatherings. And it wasn't because I was becoming a bigger customer of his either. He has run interference for me with Kari's dad on more than one occasion. I was looking forward to tomorrow now, thanks to him.

"You heard the man, cap'n. He'll send that video to the Coast Guard. Could end up costin' me any chance of getting' my captain's license down the way." Bonner's mate was trying to reason with him during their ride back to the dock.

Bonner was still incensed, and now he took it out on his mate. "I heered what he said. I guess you'd run home with your tail 'tween your legs. Not me. An Smitty was behin' this, at least partly. You seen him runnin' with those boys, but none of the rest've them Yankees did. So, I got an idea. Somethin' I gotta do before we leave. An' we leave when we're damn good an' ready; not before." The look on his face after that didn't reassure his mate one bit.

Chapter 16

The next day when we got to Kari's parent's house Carlton was out on the back deck with her father. It was warm for Thanksgiving, but still not all that comfortable outside. However, it was about the only private place left at the house since her sisters, brothers in law, uncle and a few cousins had all gotten there before us. Hopefully I wasn't the subject of their conversation, but I wouldn't bet money on that. This wasn't paranoia or ego on my part, but a logical conclusion based on similar past experiences. Fortunately, like I said, Carlton was an advocate for me.

The two of them soon finished their conversation, and her dad made a beeline for me when he came in. See, I told you I'm not paranoid.

"Denton, why don't you grab two beers and meet me out on the deck."

I did as requested, then handed him one of the bottles as I settled into a deck chair across the table from him.

"I saw that video of you getting laid out on the docks."

"You and the rest of the world." Where was he going with this?

He laughed. This was the first time laughter was involved in any conversation between us, but of course, it came at my expense.

"At first I was embarrassed for you, needing your buddies to take that guy out. Then I saw the whole tape and realized you were sucker-punched by him. You've got some pretty loyal friends, and I'm related to more than a few of them." He glanced through the window where Carlton and his brother Billy, the sheriff of Accomack County, were deep in conversation and looking in our direction.

"To be honest with you, I haven't had that much experience with fighting over my lifetime, though I've never backed away from one either."

He grunted, "Not much of a waterman."

"I didn't know that was a requirement for being one." I was already starting to get my back up. I respect him because I'm at his house and he is my fiancée's father, but that only goes so far.

"I meant that as a compliment. At first, I thought you were just another dock rat who wouldn't ever amount to much, but I have to admit, you've surprised me. That's not something that happens often."

I shrugged, "I didn't think I was all that hard to figure out."

"Yeah, well, I heard you'd been having a few problems out on the water lately. And I also heard that you solved 'em. That surprised me, and how you did it surprised me. I'm glad you weren't dumb enough to get suckered into another fight with that guy."

"You don't get loyal friends without being loyal to them yourself. And you don't win anything by bringing a knife to a gunfight. When somebody hits you then you better find a way to hit back even harder, and you need to win when you do. It's the only way to be sure they'll think twice before they try it again."

He paused, then cocked his head slightly, giving me a look of appraisal. "I have to admit, Denton, when Kari brought you home, I didn't like you much."

"You made that pretty clear."

"I'm not finished. I didn't like you much because I had some high hopes for her and wanted her to have a good life with a good man who has a future. Someone who also could protect and take care of her. None of that has changed. Back then I didn't think you were the man for the job. I thought you were gonna break her heart and wreck her future. You have no idea how upset it made me at the time when she went against my advice to dump you and move on. I had you pegged as just another waterman. Like I said, I'm not wrong often, but I think maybe I was then. At least I hope you'll prove that I was. So, the reason I asked you out here is because I'm giving you my blessing to marry my daughter."

Yeah, I was surprised. Would I have married Kari without his permission? Of course. I had planned to. But this will sure make things easier at more of these holiday meals. As far as I knew, I was the only prospective son-in-law he had ever approved of.

"Thanks, Mr. Denton."

"Sam. So, when are you two thinking of getting married?"

"We hadn't given it a lot of thought yet."

"Well then start thinking, Denton. It doesn't look good, you two living together, even in that nice houseboat that you both paid for. I was wrong about that, too. I thought she was on the hook for it by herself and you were just freeloading. Sorry I misjudged you, Denton."

"Marlin."

He looked confused for a second then said, "Oh, right. Marlin. Well, let's get back inside. And you two get to work on that date."

"I'll tell her. She'll pick it; you know how organized she is. She'll plan it all then tell me when to be there."

"You know something Marlin, you're getting smarter by the minute."

"Really? Daddy said that?"

We were in my truck on the ride back to Mallard Cove. This was the first time we'd had a chance to talk in private since my conversation with her dad. Frankly, I hadn't thought a lot about wedding plans; I'd kind of had my hands full, as you know. But the look on Kari's face right now was worth everything her father had put me through, or rather had put us through, over this past year. It was excitement mixed with relief. She idolized her dad and I guess it had been weighing heavily on her that she had gone against his wishes. Somehow I'd missed seeing how much that had affected her. Yes, I know she's twenty-five, and has her own mindset about things. Except when she's around her dad, then she becomes his little girl again.

"Un huh. Told me to call him Sam, too."

"You know he's never done that with any of my sisters' husbands, right?"

"I never really thought about it."

"Trust me, Marlin, that's huge. It's more than I ever hoped for. It's not just you that he approves of, it's *us*. It means he believes in me again, as well as my decisions. I'm so happy right now! May twenty-seventh."

"Hmm?"

"We'll get married on May twenty-seventh."

No, she didn't even need to look at a calendar, she's got that kind of memory. "Okay. Wait, you mean this coming year?"

"No, ten years from now. Of course this coming year!"

We'd be in final post-production for *Tuna Hunters* and getting set to film the first show of the new series. I said hesitantly, "Okay."

As if reading my mind she said, "They'll live without you for two weeks."

"Wait, *two weeks?*"

"Lots to do beforehand including the rehearsal, rehearsal dinner, wedding, and of course a honeymoon in Bermuda. And you'll need a best man and four groomsmen. Just give me the list and I'll get them set up with tuxedo rental fittings. We'll work together on guest lists for the wedding and the rehearsal dinner."

My head was swimming. "Want to elope instead?" The look I got instantly said I was nuts for even bringing up such an absurd idea. But hey, it was worth a shot. I was finding out the old adage was true; weddings are for and all about the women. Guys should just go with the current and follow along. If they're smart, that is.

"Please tell me that you'll be back by May," Kari asked. We had gone straight over to Murph and Lindsay's houseboat when we got back to Mallard Cove.

Lindsay looked at her questioningly, "Early March. We decided not to be gone as long this winter. Why?"

"Because I'm going to need your help. We're getting married on May twenty-seventh, and I'd love it if you'd be my Maid of Honor."

Lindsay's reaction was to vault out of her chair over to Kari, gathering her up in a big hug. "Of course I will! This is fantastic news, isn't it Murph?"

"I guess so. Should be a heck of a party, if nothing else."

I was relieved that I wasn't the only guy around here that didn't go all gaga over weddings.

"Uh, something I need to ask you, Murph. Stand up for me as Best Man?"

He grinned widely, "Do I get to plan the bachelor party?"

"You bet."

"Oh, heck yes, I'm in! This is going to be epic!"

"Just make sure you get him to the wedding in one piece, babe. Hungover is fine, but conscious enough to say, 'I do' is a must." Lindsay knew the two of us all too well.

"Will do. Speaking of which, this calls for drinks so we can toast the big event. I'm making vodkas for everybody."

Trust me, it was all about the drinks with Murph, not the "big event." And the four of us have been known to hurt ourselves on vodka, but since they were leaving in three days, it was an appropriate choice. Beer just wouldn't do right now. Besides, all this talk about planning was giving me a headache and I needed a real drink. I wished that Murph and Lindsay wouldn't be leaving for so long, they were the pals I could always lean on. They were both closer than siblings to me. Now that I was so totally out of my element with all this wedding stuff, I'd need their advice, and I was bummed that they would be gone the next three-plus months. I just hoped that I would stay busy with the shows up until then.

Two drinks later we all headed up to the *Cove Restaurant* where we had Thanksgiving dinner all set for our friends, cast, and crew that didn't have any family close by. Smitty, Peter Newman, Brittany Newman, Mack James, and Angie James were the only ones here from the northern crew. Spud, Bill, and Betty were it from our local crew, along with a half dozen of the production company's staff including Tracy Brill. She had started heading for me when she ran into Kari. A few minutes later I saw Tracy talking with Brittany Newman, then she headed my way again.

"Marlin, can I have a word with you outside?" She looked perturbed.

"Sure?" I wondered what was up as we went out onto the deserted and cold deck that overlooked charter boat row.

"What happened offshore yesterday?"

Not a lot of people would have questioned their boss this way. But I knew that she had a deep concern for all the crews and lately, specifically for Spud.

"We put a stop to Banner and company's harassment."

"By *sinking* him?"

"We didn't plan on sinking him. Frankly, I'm not exactly sure what happened there, it might have something to do with his boat being so old, I don't know."

The depth of her anger was starting to surface now, "You told me that protecting fisheries wasn't worth compromising anyone's safety. That no television show would ever be worth endangering lives. I believed you, and I believed *in* you. But I meant about not putting anyone out on the water at risk, not just our cast. Apparently, you didn't."

Now it was my turn to get upset. "Dammit, Tracy, I did, and I still do. By doing what we did we were trying to protect our people. Bonner and his pals were getting more and more reckless out there, and it was only a matter of time until someone got seriously hurt or worse. I don't want anyone else to have to go through what you have been and are still going through. Remember that Spud was in our cockpit when Bonner was racing by close enough for me to toss a fly line across his bow. And do you know why we call Kim Collier "Hard Rock"? Because he ended up on the rocks at one of the tunnel islands when his steering gear failed. Obviously with that rickety old rig of Bonner's the same thing could've happened, and then there would've been no way for him to stop before he was into our cockpit and on top of everyone in it.

"We warned them numerous times and told them we wouldn't be held responsible if they didn't stop. Remember, they were trying to force us into moving the show back south, and nobody is more aware than you about how that inlet is a hundred times more dangerous than ours. So, I *was* trying to protect my people, *our* people. And by doing so I was also protecting Bonner's crew, at least that was the idea.

"I meant every word I told you; nothing has changed about that. Am I sorry that Bonner's boat sank? Yes, though I'd be lying if I said I didn't find a little bit of pleasure in that whole karma thing. But in the end I'm glad he won't be around here anymore. Remember, I wasn't the one who traveled two hundred miles to pick a fight in his backyard like he did in ours."

She mulled that over for a minute. "I can see your point, but I'm just sorry it came to that."

160

"I am too. But knowing what I know now, I'd still do it again if I thought that was the only way I could get them to stop. And it was." I looked her square in her eyes, "So, are we good?"

She thought for a minute then nodded. "Yes. We're good. The truth is that I'd have also done whatever it took to make sure everyone was safe. Even more than you did if the situation called for it, so I guess I can't fault you. But I wasn't sure what had motivated you or what you had intended to do."

"Well, now you are. Tracy, I feel a heavy responsibility for every single member of the cast and crew, you included. I don't want you or anyone else to have any doubts about that."

"Thank you, Marlin, that's something we share." She leaned her head to the side a bit, "On a much lighter note, I hear you and Kari have set a date for your wedding. Congratulations."

I chuckled, "Word travels fast around here." I was glad we were now past the trust issues. Again.

"Yes, we're like a small town in that respect," she said.

We turned to go back inside and I saw Brittany Newman had been watching us from inside the glass doors. As we started in her direction she came outside and headed in ours.

"Can I talk to you, Tracy?" She ignored me like I wasn't even there, which I thought was curious since she had always been friendly to me before. I nodded at her as I went inside, leaving them to talk in private. The nod wasn't returned.

"He's just like Lorne, doing whatever it takes to make a buck no matter who gets hurt in the process. It isn't fair Tracy; he and Kari are getting married and are going to have all that money coming in, enjoying their perfect little life. But you and I lost Jerry and Jason, and I lost my mom along the way, too. Jason and I were

161

planning for a future together like Kari and Marlin, and that's all gone now because of Lorne."

Mack and her mother had split up over the stress and hours of the show back when they had worked out of Carolina. It had strained their relationship as well, since Brittany chose to continue working on the boat with her dad. She and her mom were no longer on speaking terms.

"That's what we were just talking about, Brittany. It turns out that sinking *Voodoo* was just an accident; they still don't know what happened. I believe that Marlin had all our best interests at heart when he went up against Bonner. He wasn't intentionally trying to hurt him, he just wanted to get him to pack up and leave. And you're wrong about him and Kari getting the money from the show, they don't take a dime from it. All the profits go directly to MAFF."

Brittany fumed, "And he gets paid from MAFF. What difference does it make if it comes from one hand or the other? It's still why he wanted the show, and from what I heard, he got it for next to nothing. Don't let him con you, Tracy, it's about the money. He needed Bonner out of the way so that he wouldn't interrupt the filming and the precious cash flow."

Since they had become so close after their shared tragedy, Tracy already knew there would be no reasoning with Brittany until after she cooled down. She also knew that a lot of this was about Marlin and Kari getting married; Brittany was envious that they had a future together. Brittney believed the show, and more specifically Lorne, had taken away her only chance for a similar life. A life that died when Jason did. In her mind, Marlin had just replaced Lorne in every way, and this incident with Bonner had reaffirmed that for her. Tracy knew this was the real trigger, and it was best to let her younger friend calm down on her own.

"Let's go back inside, have a drink and relax."

162

"I don't want to. Tell my dad I wasn't feeling well, and that I went back to the boat to lie down, would you? Ask him to bring me a plate when he comes back."

Tracy watched Brittany walk toward B Dock in the growing dusk, then went back inside to be with the rest of the group.

Chapter 17

Just as we were all finishing our meal, Spud pointed out the window and yelled, "Fire!"

In the darkness, we could see the orange and yellow reflection of flame in the space between two of the charter boats. Something, or rather some *boat* was on fire over on B Dock.

"It's *Sea Quest*! And I left Thor in the cabin!" Smitty jumped up and rushed out the door, followed by the rest of our group. By the time we reached the boat, the cockpit was completely engulfed, along with the wheelhouse bulkhead and the cabin sides. Smitty jumped on the bow, forcing open the forward hatch. Smoke came billowing out as Smitty yelled his dog's name but got no response.

I jumped on the foredeck beside Smitty, took one look at the hatch and the smoke and said, "I can fit through there easier than you." With that, I took a deep breath and lowered myself down through the hatch into the cloud of acrid black smoke. There's nothing worse than fiberglass on fire; it emits noxious and very deadly poisonous fumes and is next to impossible to put out. I couldn't see anything in the smoke-filled cabin and was holding my breath as I searched, almost completely by feel.

I explored the deck with my feet until I felt a soft something between the vee berths. Thor. He wasn't moving. I was running out of oxygen and climbed up on a bunk to stick my head out of the hatch. I paused just long enough to get a breath of what turned out to be a mixture of both air and smoke. Ducking back down I heard the windows in the wheelhouse bulkhead break. The heat was getting intense, and I could now feel rather than see the fire advancing down toward Thor and me. I was choking on the smoke mixture I had inhaled as I gathered the huge dog up, wrapping my arms around his chest just behind his forelegs. It took every ounce of strength I had to lift his head through the hatch before I felt hands reach under his forelegs to lift him up and out.

My lungs were burning, I had again reached my limit of holding my breath and coughed involuntarily. Now I inhaled an even stronger dose of that toxic smoke mixture into my lungs. I began coughing more violently, which only made me inhale more. As my head began reeling I grabbed the side of the hatchway to pull myself out, my one hand slipped. Someone grabbed my wrist below the hand that was still halfway out of the hatch, and I was lifted up and partway though. Then they grabbed my belt and yanked me the rest of the way out.

"Help me get him off of here!"

I recognized Murph's voice, but I couldn't see anything yet. My vision was blurred from the smoke and I was having a coughing jag, but I knew I was lying face down on the foredeck, and most of what I was inhaling now was smoke-free air. But the deck I was laying on was getting very hot as the space above the vee berths now became engulfed. Flames started shooting out of the open hatch. Then someone was dragging me by my wrists again, this time over to the side of the boat where they half lifted and half dropped me to the dock. Then two people were supporting me, one under each arm as they half lifted and half dragged me away. With their help, I finally began stumbling down the dock and away from the flaming Sea Quest. I was blinking, coughing, and retching as my eyes slowly cleared, though my lungs continued to protest.

"Get him over onto that dock box!"

It turned out the person on my right side was a very worried Kari. I looked back over my shoulder and could barely make out Vulture, the only boat next to Sea Quest, pulling out of her slip and away from the fire. In the distance I heard sirens, then Kari's worried face was in front of mine as I sat down on the box.

"How's. Thor?" I asked in between hacking.

Kari pointed down the dock fifteen feet away where Smitty was bent over a prone Thor, giving him mouth to snout resuscitation.

"He must've breathed in a lot of smoke, Marlin." Her face was distraught; she had gotten as attached to him as I had. "And that was by far the dumbest thing you have ever done, going into that inferno."

"Had to. Couldn't. Leave him. To die. And Smitty. Would've died trying. To. Get to him."

It was hard to talk since I was still coughing and my throat was now raw. I spit on the dock, trying to get the acrid, plastic-like taste out of my mouth. The light from the power pedestal showed that the gob was gooey and black. I must've breathed in even more smoke than I thought. Kari sat down on the box next to me, putting her arm across my shoulder as we watched Smitty continue to work on Thor.

The sirens drew closer and the fire trucks soon pulled up behind us in the parking lot. Within a minute and a half of arriving they were spraying foam on what little remained of *Sea Quest*. A fireman had hooked me up with an oxygen mask and was now helping Smitty with Thor. Gradually my coughing subsided enough to where I could pull the mask off. The entire time we watched Smitty with his pal we hadn't seen any movement from the prone white figure on the dock. Tears started streaming down my face as it hit me that despite my best efforts, I'd been too late.

"It's okay Marlin, you did everything you could've." Kari was in tears now, too. Thor had such a great personality, it was easy to forget he was a dog, and so easy to get attached to him.

Then I saw a paw twitch. "He moved!"

"What?"

We quickly went over to where Smitty was reassuring his four-pawed sidekick. "It's going to be okay, Thor. Just relax and stay down, pal."

Despite his master's instructions, Thor tried to roll over onto his stomach. But Smitty held him down, forcing him to relax and take in more oxygen from a special mask the fireman had attached to his snout. He was coughing and gagging like I had been, but his too was subsiding as the minutes went by. Kari and I were now kneeling next to him as well, stroking him reassuringly. Finally, he managed to roll over onto his belly despite Smitty's best attempts to hold him down. He shook his head, trying to dislodge the mask Smitty still held over the end of his snout. When Smitty relented, Thor licked his hand.

One of the firemen came and looked him over. "Looks like he's going to be okay. I've only seen one other pup that got caught in a boat fire. The smoke got to him and he didn't make it. This guy's lucky."

Smitty looked up and over at me, extending his huge hand for me to shake. "I owe you, Marlin, big time. Boats I can replace, but Thor's my family."

Thor seemed to understand as well, looking at me and giving me a soft "chuff".

My big friend continued, "I'm going to find out who did this, then I'm going to make them pay. Though I have a pretty good idea who it was."

I said, "You can't be sure that this was intentional. You know as much as I do that some boats just catch fire on their own. Salt water and electricity don't mix well together. Corrosion in connections has started more than just a few fires."

"True, but *Sea Quest* is barely a year old. *Was* barely a year old." He looked over at the smoldering wreck that was by some miracle still afloat. The fire had almost made it to the waterline in the cockpit which would have sunk her for certain. The batteries must still be intact since we could see the forward bilge pump's through hull fitting spewing a steady stream of foamy water the firemen used to put the fire out.

"Still, it could've been anything, Smitty," Kari agreed with me.

"Yeah it could've been, but it wasn't. I smelled the burning gasoline when we first got there. You can't mistake that smell for anything else, and *Sea Quest* has a single diesel; there wasn't any gas onboard. It's why the fire spread so fast; someone doused the cockpit and then torched her."

All the others from our dinner were now lined along the main dock, out of the firefighter's way. Brittany walked over to check on Thor, followed by Tracy. I was sure that they had been out of earshot; neither could have overheard our conversation.

"Hey Britt, did you see anyone around my boat? Or anybody or anything that seemed out of place when you headed back," Smitty asked.

"What? No! I didn't see anyone between the restaurant and here. But I went below as soon as I got back. Why? Do you think this wasn't an accident?" She looked genuinely surprised.

I was looking at Brittany, but out of the corner of my eye, I saw Tracy give her this look that bordered on disbelief. It only lasted a split second like it had been a reaction, and then it was gone. I almost thought I imagined it, but no, it had been right there on her face. Why? Tracy knew Brittany better than anyone here except for her dad. Did she really believe that she was capable of torching Smitty's rig?

Smitty said, "I can't be sure. But it makes sense to check out every angle after everything that's been happening lately."

Brittany nodded almost absentmindedly, "I guess so. Let me know if I can help."

Thoughts were now racing through my head. Maybe I had been wrong thinking Lorne's murder and the attempt to sink *Sea Quest* were unrelated. And the water contamination of the fuel tanks up north. After all, Brittany had been close by when they all happened, and no one was closer to this latest attack on Smitty's boat when it happened, too. Had that been what was behind Tracy's look? Or was there something else, something only she knew about because of her close relationship with Brittany?

"That was one of the bravest things I've ever seen anyone do, Marlin." Brittany looked straight into my eyes as she said it. This was a change from her attitude toward me since dinner.

I shrugged, "You do what you have to do. I didn't stop to think about it."

"I don't know if I could have done it. I love Thor too, but that was really hairy."

I shrugged, since there wasn't much more to be said about it; "hairy" pretty well summed it up from my standpoint as well. I looked over at Smitty who was now sitting on the dock next to Thor, staring at what was supposed to have been his winter work home. I realized that while he still had Thor, he had lost not only his boat, but all his tackle and even his clothes. The tools of his trade were now gone, just days before the opening of tuna season and the official start of filming. The shock of this new reality was setting in, and I could see that his world had imploded around him. While Thor had needed me a while ago, his master was going to need my help now almost as much.

"Smitty, you, Gary, and Thor can bunk over on *Tied Knot* with us for the time being."

He nodded. "Thanks, Marlin. I don't know how long it'll take to get my insurance company to pay out, and then I have to get another boat. No way I'll be ready for this season. Gary and I'll head back north tomorrow and regroup when we get home."

I shook my head. Smitty, Thor, and Gary are the most popular crew on *Tuna Hunters*, and there was no way our production company would want them to miss this season. "We'll find you a boat, even if you have to charter one, you can't miss the show."

"And he's not gonna. Because he can use the *Golden Dolphin* until he finds another *Quest*. But I don't have any clothes that'll fitcha big guy, that's for sure." Baloney had walked up behind Smitty, his cigar staying stationary in the corner of his mouth, a sure sign this was a sincere and heartfelt offer.

"I don't know what to say, Bill."

"Ya don't hafta say a thing. But you'll need to fill the 'fridge, 'cause I'm fresh outta beer. I'm talkin' about *Mahi's* fridge, not the *Dolphin*. You'll need to fill that one too if you want any of your own."

A fireman walked up with a deputy sheriff, asking if the marina manager was around. When Kari identified herself, the deputy asked if he could view the security camera tapes from earlier in the evening. He noticed that each dock had a camera aimed down their center. Those were recorded and available online to boat owners so they could check their boats from their homes and offices. Between the marina, restaurants, bars, and hotel, Mallard Cove had over three dozen individual cameras that recorded 24/7. Kari led the pair toward the dockmaster's office while Smitty, Thor, and I went to *Quest's* slip. After determining that she should indeed be capable of floating overnight until Smitty could arrange for a tow over to Carlton's marina, we found Gary and headed over to *Tied Knot,* bypassing the restaurant. None of us were in the mood for dessert. Vodka though was a completely different story and helped to wash the smoke taste out of my mouth.

Twenty minutes later Kari came in and I fixed her one while she told us what they had discovered.

"Somebody pulled into the marina in a small Carolina Skiff, tying up at the end of the tee behind *Coastal Dreamer*. We couldn't make out his face since he was wearing a hoodie that was cinched down, and he was wearing gloves, too. Remember, the dock cams are just for a quick check by owners to make sure their boat is still floating and as a visual deterrent to thieves, but they don't automatically zoom in.

"Whoever this was already knew about the cameras as well as their locations and made sure not to show his face. But he went directly to *Quest* and looked in through the bulkhead windows. No way he didn't see Thor. Then he emptied a Jerry jug around the cockpit and down the cabin sides. Tossed a match from the dock as he left, taking the jug with him. While we couldn't see who it was, he sure matched Bonner's height and build."

At the mention of Thor, Smitty balled up his fists and inhaled deeply. "I'm gonna find that son of a bitch and make him pay. He knew Thor was in there and he didn't care."

"Smitty, the important thing is that Thor's okay. Let the cops handle Bonner. I doubt he's going to stick around after this anyhow. He blamed us for him losing his boat, and now he's pulled the 'eye for an eye' bit. Probably on his way down the coast right now." I hoped I was right.

"He wanted to kill Thor, Marlin. No way that I'm letting this go. He shows his face around here again and he's a dead man."

If Bonner could see Smitty's face right now he would be smart to disappear. Unfortunately, I don't think that anyone has ever accused him of being overly smart.

Chapter 18

Normally I could care less about "Black Friday", but this year I was really glad that most of the shops were open early this morning. An unusually subdued Thor hung out with Kari and me after Gary and Smitty left at the crack of dawn, headed to Virginia Beach to do some clothes shopping to replace what they'd lost in the fire. I'd been told that there's a good "Big and Tall" store just across the bridge, and Smitty was about to make some salesman's month.

My four-pawed pal was still feeling a little worse for wear after last night, and my lungs weren't very happy this morning either. I still had that lingering taste of fiberglass smoke in my mouth that I couldn't shake. Kind of like the next day after smoking the most putrid cigar on earth, but times ten. I don't know how Baloney does it. Thor and I both stayed close to the couch, taking it easy.

When Smitty and Gary returned with arms filled with bags of clothing, KT and Junior were waiting for them in the salon along with Kari and me.

Smitty said, "Hey guys, I was going to give you a call this morning to see if I could pay you to tow *Quest* up to Carlton's yard to get hauled out."

KT grinned, "Nope, you can't." When Smitty looked disappointed, KT continued. "Pay us that is. We'll tow you up there for free. This shouldn't have happened, at least not here. Least we can do is help you. We may be fishing on different teams, but we fishermen still gotta stick together.

"It looks like this northeast wind will swap around to the west tonight, and we'd be better protected towing her up there tomorrow. With as little freeboard as is left now in that cockpit, we'd stand a good chance of losing her to the waves in Magothy Bay if we went today. It would be best to wait one more day."

Smitty nodded, glad to have the advantage of knowing someone with local knowledge. "I'll call Carlton and see if he can take us tomorrow."

"Already set up. We'll leave here about seven in the morning," Junior replied.

Now it was my turn. "Y'all need to go unload that stuff so we can get a move on."

Both Gary and Smitty looked confused. Smitty asked, "Where are we going?"

"I'll tell you when we get there, but we need to get started. Just trust me, it'll be worth the ride."

All seven of us piled into the Sprinter, with Thor taking up the whole rear bench seat. We had a three-hour trip ahead of us, straight up US 13 and into Maryland.

*****

At that same moment, a pair of fishing boats were in the Intracoastal Waterway just below Norfolk, headed south. With the northeast wind that was howling offshore, they had opted for running the slower but more sheltered route of the "ditch" on their way back down to Carolina. Captain Willie Carney was bringing Bonner back with him aboard his boat, the *Four Aces*. He looked over at Bonner, who had just perched in a high seat on the opposite side of the wheelhouse from him, a tall drink in hand.

"A bit early ain't it, Clint?"

Bonner glared at him, "Yeah, it's too damn early to be goin' home without mah boat." He took another long draw from a large glass of rum and ice. This was actually a refill, not the one he had originally started with. He had filled that first glass when they cast off, right at dawn.

Not wanting to rile Bonner any farther, Carney switched subjects. "Saw you 'borrow' that skiff back at the dock last night, but it wasn't there when we left."

"Yeh, well, ah needed it. An ah didn't need it found this mornin' cause of what I used it fer. Sent it idlin' over toward them islands. Shoulda ended up on the beach and they'll figger some kids took it."

Carney was both concerned and curious. "So, what did ya use it for?"

Bonner broke into a sloppy grin, "Ah burned up Smitty's boat last night and that damn dog of his, too."

"You *what*!"

Bonner waved a hand dismissively, "Relax. Wasn't nobody around the dock, an I got away clean. Can't prove nothin. Besides, he took up with them Virginians, so he had it comin'. If I cain't be in that show, he ain't about to be either. An' I always hated that damn dog. Tried to bite me once, remember? He ain't gonna bite nobody no more.

"An I ain't done with that bunch, neither. Gotta let 'em settle down a few days, but I'm goin' back up there. We ain't even yet, not by a long shot. 'Specially them Denton and Baloney sumbitches. No sir, not even close. But we're gonna be when I get through with 'em all."

Bonner's words made Carney's blood run cold. "Jeezus, Clint! You hearing yourself? You killed Thor and burned Smitty's boat? They'll know who did it! And they got those video tapes of us cuttin' their lines, too. They'll think we were all in on it together! Just leave it alone and stay the hell away from there then maybe we'll get lucky and they won't put two and two..."

Bonner had jumped up and lunged at Carney, grabbing his shirt with his free hand and leaning in until their faces were only inches apart, stopping him midsentence. "Nobody tells me what ta do, you got that? An you *are* in on it. So, just keep runnin' this damn boat south, and don't you worry 'bout where I go, an what ah do after I get there." Bonner shoved Carney back in his seat, then went back to his own.

Carney said, "I'm not telling you what to do Clint, I'm just asking you to think about it a little. Shouldn't you let everything settle down until after you get your insurance check for *Voodoo*? Might not be a good idea to do anything else to pop up on their radar, know what I mean?"

Bonner took another long sip of his rum. "That'd be right if there was gonna be a check. But I didn't have no insurance on *Voodoo*. My ex cleaned me out good last year in the divorce, an' all I had left was that boat. The damn insurance company raised the rates on me 'cause she was old and wood. I was gonna sell her after this season an' use this year's money from the show to get a fiberglass boat. Now on account a them Virginians, I got nothin' left but my truck."

Bonner glanced over at Carney and didn't like the shocked look on his face. He got up and went to sit in the fighting chair in the cockpit to finish his drink in solitude. Carney's mind was trying to absorb all that he had just heard, and he was now close to panicking. Cutting fishing lines was one thing, but arson and killing a man's dog was way more than he had signed up for. And the crazy bastard was now talking about going back to do more damage.

When they started out for Virginia, Carney had hoped there was still a chance they could get back on the show. Bonner had done a sales job on all of them, making them believe it was a sure thing if they followed along and did what he said. Instead, the only sure thing left was that they were never going to be on that show or any other show ever again, thanks to what Bonner had done and talked them into. He couldn't wait to get back home, get Clint off his boat and the hell away from him. They were through.

*****

Three hours later I turned onto a curving side road which led us past several small marinas and fish houses. Not to be confused with yacht marinas, these places were home to working boats, just like the working men and women that ran them. Here at midday, many of the slips were empty, as I knew they would be since there's no such thing as a four day holiday for watermen. After passing through a couple of fishing villages and across a narrow rickety bridge, I turned down a straight tree-lined side road that looked like it ended at the water. Two-thirds of the way down was a wide driveway on the right. The small sign next to it read simply, *Jones Boatyard and Marina*. I turned in.

Up ahead was a huge commercial-looking metal building, and to the left was a three pier marina. Now surrounding the van were numerous deadrises of varying sizes. All were similar designs to KT's and were scattered around the several acres of gravel yard, "up on the hard". This was a true mixture of two different worlds; some hulls having been outfitted as pleasure boats, and others belonged to that aforementioned workboat group. Some were getting maintenance done above their waterlines. These were easily spotted by the ladders leaning against their hulls, providing easy access for the yard crews. Others had already been winterized and secured, their owners hunkering down in their homes and businesses, awaiting spring and the return of warmer weather. Almost all of these fell into the pleasure boat category.

KT leaned forward into the space between me and Smitty, who was occupying the shotgun seat. "I called Pete Jones this morning after I heard what happened to *Sea Quest*. After the way you acted when you ran my *Honey K*, I figured it was worth a run up here to see what's what. They're closed today for the holiday but Pete lives next door and said he'd come over and show us around."

"I really appreciate this, guys, but it's going to take a while before I'm ready to get a replacement for *Quest*. You know how insurance companies love dragging their feet. Besides, Baloney is loaning me his old boat."

I said, "First, you don't have to wait until your insurance check comes in, Tuna Hunter Productions will write you an advance against your future earnings for this season. Second, that was mighty generous of Bill, but would you be all that comfortable borrowing the *Golden Dolphin*? She's got a ton of hours on those old engines and if you blow one, you'll be on the hook for replacing it. That money would then be gone. And finally, third, we all saw how you looked when you ran the *Honey K*, and how you've looked at her ever since. What's it going to hurt to look around?"

He saw my logic and nodded, no further arm twisting necessary. I knew that as the highest-earning cast member he should be able to afford the new boat but I didn't know how liquid his funds were. I wanted to eliminate that hurdle. We pulled up to the office at the corner of the building as a golf cart with a single rider drove up then parked beside us. A fiftyish looking Pete Jones hopped out. After saying hello to the Williams brothers he introduced himself to Kari, Smitty, Gary, and me. He took us into the building which turned out to be a huge enclosed boatbuilding shed with a half dozen fiberglass boats in assorted sizes and various stages of completion. The overwhelming smell of fresh polyester resin assaulted our senses the second we walked through the door. I love that smell and have ever since I was a kid, but after last night it made me a little queasy right now.

Pete led us over to each of the boats, allowing Smitty to see the rugged construction of these beautiful rigs, from their bare hulls all the way to close to being ready to launch. If he hadn't been in love with these boats before this, he was completely smitten now.

177

"I wish I had the time to wait and have you build one for me, Pete."

"I wouldn't have had you rush up here today if I thought you had that kind of time, Smitty. KT told me what happened, and the spot you're in. Come on down to the dock."

We walked over to the center dock where an almost perfect clone of KT's forty-two footer occupied the second slip out. When I say "almost" I mean she's identical right down to the outriggers, with the only exception being this one's hull is maroon colored. Pete took us on board.

"I finished this one six months ago for a fellow down in Virginia Beach. Two months ago he went on vacation in the Dominican Republic and caught some kind of virus. Died a few days later in a hospital down there. His widow has asked me to sell it for her. She's not hurting for money, but her husband was the boater in the family and having it around was a painful reminder to her that he's gone. This one's got next to no hours on her, that Caterpillar engine is barely even broken in. Sips fuel at trolling speed as well as at cruise. KT said you've run his, and if you're interested we can take this one out."

That's how Smitty ended up with his latest *Sea Quest*. Pete hauled her out with his Travelift as soon as we got back in from an hour-long sea trial, letting Smitty check out everything below the waterline. They cut a very fair deal right then since the widow had given Pete the authority to negotiate for her, and he even deducted part of his commission in return for having his company's logo sticker featured on the bulkhead window. Pete is a big fan of the show, as are a lot of his customers and potential customers and he knows the value of advertising.

The yard crew was now set to change the name first thing on Monday, then Smitty and Gary will come back up and stay aboard overnight so they can run her to down to Mallard Cove on Tuesday morning. If all goes according to plan, they'll have a few hours of daylight to finish getting her ready and get some shuteye before the start of the season on Wednesday. It will be cutting it close, but it should work.

Kari and I woke up late the next morning to find Smitty, Gary, and Thor missing, then I remembered they were meeting KT and Junior to haul the old *Sea Quest* up at Carlton's. After puttering around *Tied Knot* for a few hours, Kari and I went up to the Cove for a leisurely late lunch topped off with a few beers. We had just finished our last mugs when I spotted the guys unloading the van. As they passed by on the dock, I could see they were loaded down with six new tuna rods and a dock cart filled with tackle. Thor was leading the way back to *Tied Knot*.

I told Kari, "Better order another beer, and drink it slowly."

She looked at me questioningly, "Why?"

"I've got a few thousand yards of reasons why, and they'll all need to be cranked onto those reels they came back with. If we wait until they get into a rhythm of doing that, then we shouldn't get drafted into it."

"I thought you wanted to help them?"

I replied, "I do, and I have. But filling reels the size of fifty-five-gallon drums isn't on my list of favorite things to do. I hate changing line on my reels, and they're tiny compared to those things. But if you don't want another beer..."

Kari raised her empty mug in the air and across the room our server nodded. I grinned.

"Hi, guys!" Kari and I walked into the salon on *Tied Knot* to find Smitty and Gary hard at work on their new tackle. Gary had on gloves and was sitting in a chair, holding a huge spool of fishing line while keeping

179

friction on it to make it wind tight on the reel. Smitty was sitting on the couch, dealing with the business end of a 130-pound class rod and reel combo, furiously cranking away. The reel was only about half full. Three other combos lay on the deck, already loaded up and ready for Wednesday. Another pair with empty reels waited next to them for their turns to be filled.

"You're just in time, Marlin. These three have just about worn me out. How about cranking those last two for me?" Smitty asked.

Damn it, I knew we should've ordered another round. Out of the corner of my eye, I saw Kari try to hide a smirk, knowing exactly what I was thinking right now, as she continued into our stateroom and quietly closed the door. I was sure I hadn't heard the last of this; I knew that I was in for a ribbing later. And she was in for some grief herself, for abandoning me like this.

"Sure, Smitty, I'd be happy to." Okay, I lied. Sometimes you have to do that with friends, though I try not to make it a habit. A couple more mugs of beer and I wouldn't have had to, dang it.

"Great! Because I hate doing this. The only time I want to crank this much is when there's a tuna at the other end of the line instead of Gary."

Smitty finished up that fourth reel then I took his place on the couch as he threaded line onto that next combo. Then it was off to the races as I cranked away.

"I really appreciate what you guys all did for me; from arranging this morning's tow and haul out to setting up my appointment with Pete Jones. And especially for advancing me the cash so I could get the new boat. Not to mention saving Thor, plus you and Kari putting the three of us up when we were homeless. That was a sick feeling, watching my boat go up in flames, and having no place to stay down here," Smitty said.

I shook my head, "You were never without a place to stay, and shouldn't have even needed an invitation. Just so you know in the future, you guys always have a place here if you ever need it again. I'm just glad none of the three of you were hurt.

"The tow and taking you up to Jones' were all KT and Junior's ideas. And not taking anything away from Baloney's offer, but there's nothing like fishing from your own boat with your own equipment. From a production point of view, we wanted you guys as comfortable as possible and fishing from *Sea Quest*. That's so you could be yourselves on camera, just like your fans have come to expect you to be."

Smitty's phone rang, interrupting our conversation. I got back to concentrating on winding the line evenly while Smitty did a lot of listening. After he hung up he looked worried.

"What's up," I asked.

"That was the detective assigned to our case. They located a stolen skiff beached on an island up in Magothy Bay. It had come from a small marina across from there where Bonner and friends had been tied up. They all left yesterday, headed back south. The sheriff down in Carolina just missed him by a couple of hours this morning. He cleaned out his bank account and disappeared, they don't even know which direction he was headed in when he left. He could easily be headed back here."

I had stopped winding. "If he is, he'll find quite a reception waiting for him. I'll warn everyone to keep their eyes out and their weapons handy. He shows up here and we'll all be waiting on him."

Chapter 19

Kari and I had one last dinner with Murph and Linds on Saturday night before they left on Sunday. Over dinner, they told us they were debating about leaving a few days later and hanging around to help watch our backs, at least until filming starts on Wednesday. Their thinking was that if Bonner was going to do something, it would be between now and then. We insisted they still head out the next morning. They had a thousand miles of coastline to cover and a lot of variables between here and south Florida. Weather, mechanical issues, any one of a dozen things could affect their arrival date. And they had tournament charter clients depending on them. They finally and very reluctantly agreed to stick to their original schedule.

On Sunday morning just before dawn Kari and I were dockside, handing Lindsay the lines and fenders as she and Murph pulled out. I hated this part because even though Baloney and the rest of the crew were still here, the place seems empty without Murph and Linds. Kari and I stood on the rip rap breakwater, watching their running lights grow smaller and smaller until they finally passed out of sight beyond Fisherman Island. Then Kari and I headed over a little early to our usual Sunday morning breakfast table and stack of newspapers at the *Cove*.

You know by now that I tend to over-analyze things, and this situation is no exception to that rule. We had yet to have any new Bonner sightings. And I was beginning to hope that he had headed south for the winter like so many other boats and crews. But something kept nagging at me; that little alarm bell in the back of my head was ringing non-stop. It still felt like he wasn't done with us yet, though I couldn't put my finger on the reason why. But Kari and I were both carrying our Glocks now everywhere we went, even when we were only walking across the parking lot to our offices.

All through breakfast I had silently been rationalizing that since Bonner had looked through the bulkhead window of *Sea Quest*, he hadn't been out to hurt anyone. It was more likely that he just wanted to cost them money and time. And maybe he hadn't known that Thor was aboard since Smitty took him with him almost everywhere. Then again, I knew that Thor was finely attuned to that boat and would've been up and at attention the second he felt, heard, or sensed someone coming aboard. No, seeing someone peering through the tinted bulkhead windows, there is no way he wouldn't have been barking his head off.

So, Bonner knew that Thor was in there. He had targeted him just as much as he had *Sea Quest*. And how far of a jump was it from killing a dog to killing a human? For many, it would be too far, but the more I thought about it I doubted Bonner would hesitate to kill me if the proper opportunity presented itself. All the *Tuna Hunters* boats and crews were targets, and from what he shouted at me as his boat was sinking, I was his biggest target of all.

"Did you see what Baloney did to the *Dolphin*?" Smitty asked. He and Greg walked up to our table as Kari motioned for them to sit with us. I was glad, since I needed the distraction. I also knew where Smitty was headed with that comment.

I said, "It's the official first sign of the holiday season."

Every year right after Thanksgiving, Bill secures an inflatable Santa Claus to the top of the tuna tower with an empty beer can glued in its hand. A pair of floodlights illuminates the scene, ensuring it can be seen over the *Cove's* roof as far away as the last bridge span of the CBBT.

Gary laughed, "He's one of a kind. We've got some wild characters up north, but nobody quite like him."

Kari replied, "You should be here in the summer when the wahoo are running. Instead of a pennant, he flies a black brassiere on his outrigger for every one they catch. He gets a lot of attention for our charter dock. The wahoo bit has even been in a few fishing magazines. You're right, he's one of a kind."

Smitty said, "Wait until the first show airs. You'll have to break out the big checkbook for next season, Marlin. He'll have agents lining the dock for their shot at representing him. He's going to be really popular and being popular pays."

I had already figured that Baloney's rate would go up next year if he became a fan favorite, and Smitty's comments only reinforced the thought. While I was glad for him, I wasn't looking forward to dealing with another group of agents. But I knew that all the Virginia crews would have representation next year. By then we would know who were the most popular ones, and like Smitty said, they were going to be hounded. Hey, I was the one who wanted to help them, and as the old saying goes, "Be careful what you wish for because you might just get it." I had from now until the launch of the new show season to steel myself for what lay ahead.

*****

Bonner opened his eyes, trying to focus on the room around the bed where he lay. The details came to him slowly; he remembered that he was in some fleabag motel just south of the Virginia line. He'd been here for two or three days he wasn't sure which, waiting for things to cool down. The whole world felt fuzzy, his mouth was dry, he had a serious case of skull cramps and the shakes. Over on the table by the window was a dead "handle" of cheap rum, with a more healthy-looking twin alongside it plus a plastic ice bucket. An empty pizza delivery box from who knew when was balanced halfway off the table edge.

Moving slowly Bonner checked the ice bucket finding only a shallow puddle of cool water in the bottom. Not quite trusting himself yet to be able to make the full roundtrip to the office for more, he poured two fingers of the warm brown liquid into a cheap plastic motel cup and downed it. The burning in his throat lasted only a minute before he felt the effects start to kick in. A few minutes more and then the jackhammer in his head had subsided enough to start laying out a plan for the rest of the day. At least he was pretty sure it was day since there was light coming in around the curtains over the only window. He looked at his watch, it was almost two.

He figured it was probably three hours to Mallard Cove where it would start to get dark about six. He planned to camp in his truck in the woods behind the marina, and he'd still need enough daylight to find his way back in there after he arrived. The shakiness also having subsided temporarily, he grabbed the remaining rum and headed for his truck. A note that had been stuck in the doorframe fluttered to the floor, a reminder from the manager to stop at the office to prepay another night. Bonner read it, snorted, then wadded it up and threw it on the ground next to his truck. He closed the room door, leaving the "Do Not Disturb" sign still hanging from the knob. He had a lot of ground to cover, but first he was going to need lots of carbohydrates and some ice.

*****

I watched as the new *Sea Quest* headed in on Tuesday afternoon. She was just clearing Fisherman Inlet bridge but there was no mistaking that maroon hull for any other, no matter the distance. I walked over to their slip to help Smitty and Gary tie up. From the smile on Smitty's face, I knew that he was more than pleased with his new rig.

"Marlin, this may be the best boat I've ever owned. I can't wait to get her offshore and on the tuna tomorrow."

I replied, "I'm glad that we didn't push you in the wrong direction. Carrington said that once you get a boat on your mind, you usually end up with it."

Smitty smiled. "He can read me too well. But in this case, I'm glad he did. Now we just have to load that new tackle, get our clothes off of *Tied Knot* and pick up a few things at the store and we'll be ready. New season, new boat, and now some good luck." He paused, his smile disappearing. "Speaking of luck, I talked to the detective again on the way down. Bonner's vanished. He said that we all need to keep an eye out. The other detective in Carolina talked with the captain he rode back south with. Bonner was drinking heavily the whole trip and threatening all of us here. He said that he told him he didn't have insurance on *Voodoo*, and he's now all but broke. Meaning he's not somebody that has anything left to lose."

I replied, "Which makes him very dangerous."

He nodded. "Yeah, even more than usual. Not that anything about that dude was ever not dangerous."

"I'll remind everyone about that tonight at the kickoff dinner. Don't forget, all cast and crew need to be up at the *Fin and Steak* at six." I had been looking forward to tonight, but now I wasn't happy about having to share the detective's warning. But it came with the territory.

A little after five Bonner pulled into a seldom-used road leading back into the woods north of Mallard Cove. Calling it a road was generous; it was more like two muddy ruts in an overgrown trail. Bonner followed the meandering trail to a fork, then took the one that led south. It ended in a small clearing where Bonner got out and took a short hike back through the trees. Quickly he found himself at the property line with a great view of the rear of Spud's bait shop and part of the marina.

Now that he knew his way here, he needed to get back to the truck. The first order of business was another drink to kill off the shakiness that had started to return. After that, he had a case of a dozen empty liquor bottles to fill with gasoline and then top off with rags. He figured he had just enough light left in the day to get this all done and bring the case of bottles back to this spot with him. Then he'd wait. He knew that the night before opening day of tuna season all the crews would be asleep by ten, and the *Cove Restaurant* behind the boats should be closed by then, too.

Bonner spotted an empty dock cart next to the bait shop which would be perfect to haul the case of Molotov cocktails over to charter boat row. He'd grab it after it was dark. Sitting next to each other in the liquor box all those rags should light together, then all he had to do was grab them one by one and lob three into each of the four Virginia boats' cockpits.

What he lacked in formal education, Bonner made up for in cunning and meanness. He had gotten his own charter boat business this way, by not letting anyone on the docks push him around. And he wasn't about to allow anyone to start now, especially Denton. He knew his plan should take out the entire Mallard Cove team tonight, burning all their boats to the waterlines. Sitting side by side, there would be no hope of putting the fires out once they all got started. And nobody would be crazy enough to want to take their places, not if they knew what was good for them. The show would be history, and it will cost Denton what it had cost him...everything. Bonner smiled at the thought, then headed back to his truck.

Chapter 20

"I want to thank all of you here tonight for several things. First, for being part of what I believe will be the most successful cast and crew ever of the *Tuna Hunters* show. And second, for putting up with such a newbie of an executive producer, namely me." I paused for a few beats to let the chuckles die down. "Carrington is going to pass out the new production rules for this year. I think you'll find that they are pretty much the same as they've been in prior years with one big exception, which I'll get to in a minute."

I paused to make sure that I had everyone's attention. "I like to sleep well at night, and I wouldn't be able to do that knowing I hadn't done everything I could to make this show and everyone involved in it as safe as possible. I know in the past many of you have been put under some intense pressure to fish in every conceivable condition. Some of which may have caused or contributed to serious accidents. That's going to stop right here and right now. I want you all to know that I feel a tremendous personal responsibility for the safety of every cast and crewmember. I want everybody coming back in from every trip just as safe as when they left.

"With that in mind, this year if the producers of this show deem that the conditions are too dangerous to be able to fish safely, we may declare a 'lay day' the same as you find in fishing tournaments." I saw Mack James and Troy Paulson both scowl. "I know that each captain has the ultimate responsibility for their boat and crew, and if you want to go anyway, that's your right. However, if you do, any fish caught that day will not be counted into the show's season total in determining the final winner, nor will they be mentioned on the show. Also, we will not be sending out any of our crew with you that day."

I let that sink in before continuing. "If you do choose to stay at the dock on a lay day I've instituted a safety bonus of two thousand dollars for each of those boats that remain docked." I saw the scowls then soften quite a bit. Tracy and Brittany were seated together, and both looked happy upon hearing this news. "It comes down to this; the safety of every one of you is worth more to me than any amount of video or even this whole show. So this year we are going to create some great television together, and we're going to do it safely. Is everyone with me?"

The applause started a split second faster from Tracy and Brittany than any others, but even Mack and Troy joined in. Smitty looked around then stood up.

"Guys, this is the difference that having a true fisherman at the helm makes. Marlin has been out there making a living himself, and he knows what we all do. In keeping with what he's doing, how about all of us in the Calcutta agree that if anybody does decide to go out on a lay day, any fish caught then don't count toward that total, either. Captains raise your hands if you agree," Smitty said.

I looked around as eight hands went up, though some raised slower than others. But in the end, it was unanimous. And for the record, I didn't put Smitty up to this, he did it on his own. Maybe it had something to do with losing his boat and almost losing Thor, but more likely it was just Smitty being Smitty and he'd have done it no matter what.

After dinner was over, Kari, Smitty, and I were standing around talking when Brittany, Tracy, and Spud came up to us. These past few days I'd noticed that Tracy and Spud had been going a lot of places together.

Brittany said, "Marlin, I'm sorry. I had misjudged you from the start. I had thought that you were just another Lorne, and I was wrong. Thank you for what you did tonight."

"You, too, Smitty. I know that wasn't popular with everybody," Tracy said.

Smitty shrugged, "Maybe. But it was the right thing to do after Marlin stepped up and put the show's checkbook on the line like he did. I couldn't leave things hanging like that. Now nobody's as tempted to do stupid stuff."

I put a reassuring hand on Brittany's shoulder and got a smile for the effort. Hopefully, the whole lay day idea will now put some worries behind her.

"Well, I've got a fur pal that will need a final walk before I turn in, so I'll see you guys tomorrow, bright and early," Smitty said.

Brittany asked, "Hey, I'll go walk him for you, Smitty, then you don't have to rush out. It's the least I can do in return for what you just said and did."

"Done deal. Besides, Thor loves you and he'll enjoy walking with you."

Brittany left, heading for B Dock.

"I've got some baits soaking in a super-secret brine that I've been working on. I need to rig them up over at the shop and drop 'em off over at *Double M*," Spud said.

"*Double M*," I asked?

"*My Mahi*. I'm messing with Baloney. He hates it when I call the new boat that."

I chuckled. "I'm filing that one away for future use. Mind if I take a look at those baits? After all, I'm not fishing against you."

"C'mon over. Just forget about any ingredients you might see lying around."

I said, "Trust me. Besides, I get all my baits from you anyway. Maybe I can talk you out of some of these if they work out."

Spud and Tracy left, heading for his shop together. Yep, there was something going on there, he doesn't invite just any woman to his bait shop after hours. And it takes a special kind of woman to want to see a new secret weapon bait brine. Not exactly the best pickup line ever invented. Who knows, maybe those two have a future together. Each could do far worse.

A couple of minutes later, Smitty, Kari, and I walked over to the base of B Dock. Smitty split off, heading for his boat while Kari and I kept going toward the bait shop. Then all hell broke loose.

*****

Bonner lugged the case Molotov cocktails to the edge of the woods in total darkness, colliding with a few trees in the process. It wasn't until he got closer to the edge of the woods that the lights of Mallard Cove began penetrating the thicket and helped him with tree avoidance. He paused just inside the edge of the woods, watching for anyone that might be around on the docks. Fortunately, it was a cold night, one better spent indoors than out, so there wasn't a soul in sight. Even so, he planned to wait another hour before attacking, sometime around ten, just to be certain not to run into anyone. In the meantime, he was going to steal the dock cart, bring it over to the tree line and load it with the case of bottles.

He saw the cart was still where he had spotted it a while ago, over by the bait shop. One more scan of the area and then he crouched low, quickly making his way across the open space between it and the woods. He was pretty certain that he wouldn't be in view of any of the security cameras on this side of the building. Just in case though he cinched down the edge of his hoodie, the same one he wore the night he burned Smitty's boat.

As he approached the cart outside of the screened processing room, he heard voices approaching from over by the docks. Panicking, he turned and started to retrace his steps but realized that as fast as the voices were approaching, he'd never make it back to the trees before being spotted. If that happened, he was screwed. His only chance was to hide in the screened room until these people passed by. He tried the side door and to his relief, it wasn't locked. Silently he slipped inside, his eyes adjusting enough to what little light was spilling through the screens from the marina. He could just make out the shapes of several processing tables and barrels. He slipped between the back screen wall and a table in the darkest corner. He silently swore over both his predicament and the fact that he hadn't brought his rum drink with him.

Lately, Spud had been having the time of his life. His business had grown quite a bit over the summer, and after the new season of *Tuna Hunters* gets released with all of that extra exposure, it should go nuts. He knew Baloney and Marlin had saved his butt this winter by adding him to the show, keeping him from having to let Andrea go for the slow season.

Yet it was Tracy that had been a big part of his happiness lately. Yeah, she had brushed him off at first, then all that changed after he laid out Bonner. He went from being the pursuer to the pursued in less than an hour. Go figure. But he wasn't about to question a good thing. You'd have to go a long way to find such a classy and pretty lady who was okay with going out with a bait shop owner and part-time fishing mate. Especially a lady who was as nice to talk with as she was. And smart about business, too. He didn't know exactly where this was heading, all he knew was he was happy right now and that was good enough.

She had taken his arm as soon as they walked outside, and she kept it all the way to the front door of the bait shop. On the way over she had been talking about how happy she was about the new safety rule. She stopped short of saying that if it had been in place from the first day of *Tuna Hunters*, her husband and son would still be alive. Spud knew she probably felt that way, and he understood. It was part of what continued to draw him to her.

Spud unlocked the front door and turned on the shop lights. He gathered his rigging tools and asked her to grab them a couple of beers from the display cooler. Then he headed out the side door that led into the screened rigging room, turning on those lights before setting his knives, needles, floss, and the sharpening stone on one of the rigging tables. He grabbed a dip net then bent over to retrieve his latest experimental baits before the world exploded in white light that quickly turned to black.

"Spud, I grabbed a couple of Dogfish Head Ales because I thought with fish in the name it might be good luck for tomorrow," Tracy said.

She was coming through the doorway with the two bottles when she saw Spud laying on the floor, a piece of sharpening stone on the concrete on either side of him. Bonner was standing over Spud but now staring at her. She screamed. He lunged and caught her by one of her wrists as she kept screaming. She swung the bottle in her free hand at his head but he deflected it with an arm.

Tracy kept swinging and screaming and Bonner knew he had to shut her up. He saw Spud's rigging tools on the table next to her and grabbed the closest sharp instrument, one of the long rigging needles. She swung again and partially connected with his head, coming close to stunning him. But he had simultaneously plunged the sharp end of the ten-inch needle deep into her chest. Tracy stopped screaming and started gasping, dropping both bottles.

The side door burst open as Thor and Brittney charged in. Thor instantly recognized Bonner as a threat to both Brittney and Tracy and instinctively lunged for him, grabbing him on a leg, just above the knee. Bonner released his grip on Tracy and she fell sideways to the floor, then he started howling in agony while hitting Thor with his fists. Brittney grabbed Bonner's arms, raising them above their heads as she started screaming for help at the top of her voice.

Bonner's leg was in agony from Thor's teeth, and he knew he had to do something fast to get the dog off of him and shut Brittney up. He let go of one of her arms then grabbed a fillet knife as she connected solidly, her fist to his jaw. If he hadn't been such a dock brawler and taken many of these shots before, that hit might have stunned him. She drew back to hit him again then saw the knife. She put her arm up in defense just as the blade came down, slicing deeply through skin and muscle on her forearm. She felt sick to her stomach as the blade reached the bone. Bonner drew the knife back above his head, readying for another stab as Brittney now grabbed the wrist that held the knife. Blood was spurting from her arm and into Bonner's face. She managed to slow the arc of the blade, but despite having built up her muscles through the hard work of fishing, Bonner was just too strong for her. It was only a matter of time before he would be able to plunge the blade in her throat or chest. Their battle resembled an arm wrestling mismatch where you knew the one contestant's arm would be pinned soon, as it descended toward the table almost in slow motion. Only, this arm had a blade, and it was about to become a fight to the death. Brittney now had mere seconds to live.

*****

We heard the scream, then Kari and I instantly broke into a full sprint with Smitty not far behind, determining that it was coming from the bait rigging shack. A few seconds later the scream stopped. We were still twenty yards away when we saw Thor and Brittney reach the door and go in. A second later she was screaming for help. I don't even remember drawing my

Glock 19, I just found it in my hand as I went through the door, a split second before Kari.

What I saw in front of me was like something from a horror movie. Bonner and Brittney were turned sideways to us with Thor ripping Bonner's thigh. He was a second or two from stabbing Brittney, the knife was moving ever so slowly toward her. With no verbal warning, no thought or hesitation, my gun seemed to aim itself as I fired, again, and again, and again, my nine-millimeter hollow points all entering his right side, mushrooming, fragmenting and ripping his various internal organs to shreds. Still, he kept his hold on her with the one hand while trying to stab her with the other, his body unwilling to admit that it was already dead. Maybe it was that one and only zombie movie that I'd ever seen that prepared me for what I needed to do, but I now took quick and careful aim and put two in rapid succession into his head. This time he dropped like a stone. I let Thor keep chewing on his leg, not calling him off.

Brittney immediately knelt by Tracy, oblivious to her own injury. She was going to need a tourniquet since her arm was still spurting blood. Kari was attending to Spud, who was breathing, but unconscious. Smitty was looking in wide-eyed from the doorway.

I said, "Smitty, call 911. We need medics *now*! And go over to *Mahi*, Baloney always carries Quick Clot on his boats. Grab it and haul ass back, her arm is bad."

"Got it, Shaker. Be right back."

He took off at a scary pace for such a big man, but right now seconds counted. Over by Kari, Spud moaned. I took it as a good sign. I took my belt off to apply it as a tourniquet on Brittney's arm and saw that she was reaching for something on Tracy's chest. I saw it was the dental floss from Spud's rigging needle, and that it was buried deep.

"Don't! Leave that alone, if you pull it out you can do more damage," I said as Brittany withdrew her hand. I put my belt around her arm up by the elbow and tightened it until the blood started to slow.

Tracy's eyes were partially closed, and she was wheezing. I'm no doctor, but it didn't take a specialist to know she was in really bad trouble. She said something very faintly. I moved closer and knelt to hear her.

"Marlin, I did it. All by myself. Killed Lorne, tried to sink Smitty. Watered the tanks. Brittney didn't know anything. Didn't help."

Brittney said, "Shut up, Tracy. You don't know what you're saying!"

"I do. Everybody has to know you're not too blame. I am. For all of it." Her voice was lower now, her breathing more labored from the effort to talk. "Spud?"

I said, "Kari's tending to him, he'll be fine." For all I knew, that was a lie, but right now she needed comfort and support. She nodded in response, then closed her eyes, her face now white and wracked with pain.

It seemed like forever before Smitty returned with the Quick Clot. Brittney winced but didn't cry out when I put the patch on her arm. One tough gal, this stuff works well but feels like fire. It stopped the bleeding, but she was going to need a surgeon and fast. I looked over at Kari again who was still kneeling next to Spud. She met my glance and nodded but said nothing. I took it as a positive sign, and at that point, I needed one. Tracy was fading. I heard sirens in the distance, but I sensed that she needed to be in a hospital right now to still have a fighting chance.

Tracy opened her eyes, locking hers with mine as she spoke again even more faintly this time. "It was all me. Remember that, Marlin. Please keep them all safe. I tried. That's why."

It hit me, and I suddenly understood. "I promise, Tracy. You don't have to worry about that, I'll make sure they're all safe."

She closed her eyes again just as the paramedics and a deputy sheriff rolled up. All of us that were uninjured were ordered out of that confined space. I was happy to have them take our places and tend to our friends.

Chapter 21

It all became somewhat of a blur after we walked out of the bait shack. Kari and I ended up in the back of two sheriff's cars in handcuffs, watching as two paramedics vans with Tracy, Spud, and Brittney rolled out, Peter Newman also in the one with his daughter. Only Bonner's body, a medical examiner and several investigators remained inside by the time we were driven away, a half-hour later.

Kari and I were taken back to the sheriff's department, questioned for a couple of hours and then released without any charges being filed. It helped that Sheriff Billy Albury of the neighboring county arrived to lend us moral support. Both of our weapons were retained for ballistics, even though Kari hadn't fired hers. Our sheriff was just being thorough, especially since this was going to make the news in a big way, much bigger of course than when Bonner merely decked me.

Tracy hadn't made it, she died in the paramedic's van on the way to the hospital. The needle had punctured the aorta, letting her chest cavity fill with blood and keeping her lungs from inflating. I had been right though, if Brittany had removed the needle, she would have died even faster, though in the end it hadn't mattered.

After over an hour-long surgery, Brittney's arm had been sewn up and she wasn't expected to have any lasting physical effects from it. Mentally was another issue, after losing her good friend and surviving her fight with Bonner by only seconds. She was being kept overnight at the hospital, under sedation and with an antibiotic IV.

Spud was also being kept for observation since he had a bad concussion. Fortunately, the sharpening stone Bonner had hit him with was his old one that had been worn down almost halfway through in the middle. That was exactly where it broke after coming in contact with his skull. If it had been a new one, it might not have been the stone that did the breaking.

When we arrived back at Mallard Cove, Baloney and Smitty had taken charge of keeping everyone away from Kari and me, not letting anyone else aboard *Tied Knot*. It wasn't the first time I had taken a life, but it still wasn't easy, though both times I was in the right. I wasn't up for seeing anyone yet. Fortunately, Billy was going to talk to Kari's dad, and she would call him later in the day. We lay on top of our bed fully clothed, not saying anything, just holding each other. Not sleeping, either.

The cast had declared a "lay day" on their own, without any prompting from Carrington or me. Later that afternoon they would decide to stretch it into two days. I called Murph and Lindsay on video chat at six a.m. so they wouldn't hear about what happened from the news or anyone else. Murph said he would call the rest of Mallard Cove's partners for Kari, to let them know what happened and that we were okay.

There was no sense in laying around in bed all day, so a little before seven we got up and I made coffee for the two of us, Smitty and Baloney, too. Then we all went to the top deck. Across the basin and over top of the boats we could see there were still a couple of sheriff's cars in front of Spud's shop. After a few minutes, I had seen all I wanted to, and the cold morning air was quickly cooling my coffee. We all retreated to the galley for a warmup.

Kari excused herself to get showered and changed while Smitty went to the *Cove* to pick up breakfast sandwiches for all of us. Though I didn't feel like eating, it was a nice gesture. Baloney and I then sat in the salon while he was gone.

He asked, "You all right?"

I nodded. "I will be. Still kind of in shock. It's not any easier."

Baloney grunted. "You just focus on the part where you saved that gal's life, that's what's important. Might've saved Spud, too. We don't know what that looney-toon woulda done after he killed Brittney, might've turned the knife on Spud to finish the job. Damn glad you got there when you did, Shaker."

I laughed out loud, and Bill looked at me like I'd lost my mind. "No, Bill, it just hit me, when I sent Smitty to get the Quick Clot from you, he called me Shaker, too. First time he's ever done that."

Baloney smiled. "When I give somebody a nickname, it sticks. And him using it? Why not, he's one of us now. All those Yankees are. Last night you were protecting one of them, but this mornin' she's one of us, and will be from now on..."

Baloney kept talking, but I was stuck on what he had just said. I hadn't told the investigators all of what Tracy told me, I left part of it out, though I didn't know why I felt like I needed to at the time. I did now. Brittney and I needed to talk.

"Hey, Shaker! You still with me?" Baloney looked concerned.

"Yeah, Bill, just going over some things in my mind. Probably won't be the last time today that I zone out."

"Don't blame you a bit, pal. It's a lot to deal with. You do what you need to do."

"I think after Kari gets out of the head, I'm going to get cleaned up and go over to the office. I can't sit around here all day."

It was a good thing I did end up at the office, since Carrington was dealing with a media firestorm. It wasn't every day that a producer shoots and kills an ex-cast member who was trying to murder a current one and burn a pile of boats. A deputy had found the case of

Molovov cocktails in the woods, and had connected the dots.

By the afternoon though I was up to doing a few video interviews from our conference room. Like it or not, this publicity would boost interest in the show, and dealing with it was part of the job I had taken.

Brittney and her dad came by to thank me, her injured arm all wrapped in heavy gauze in a sling. I asked Kari to come down from her office to join us and motioned for them to sit while we waited. Kari closed the conference room door after she came in, leaving the four of us able to have a private conversation.

I started, "You know I don't believe Tracy, right Brittney?"

She squirmed in her chair, "How can you say that about Tracy, Marlin? She confessed everything because she knew she was dying, and she wanted it off her conscience."

I wasn't buying what Brittney was trying to sell. I said softly, "No, Brittney. She died doing what she had done even before her family died, and every day since. She was protecting her family. Meaning, every person that goes out on those boats to earn their living. She adopted all of you on that terrible day down in Carolina. She had been trying to convince Lorne to back off the pressure for months, but he wouldn't back down.

"Then she lost Jerry and Jason. Yet Lorne still kept up the pressure on everyone. So, she killed him before anyone else could get hurt or die. I'm guessing that at some point after you two bonded over your shared loss, she told you what she'd done."

"Just where are you going with this, Denton? Can't you see she's been through enough." Peter Newman was starting to get angry.

"Yeah, Peter, I know. Just as I know she didn't kill Lorne, but she did try to sink *Sea Quest* up north, and she put the water in all the fuel tanks."

201

Brittney scowled, "You heard Tracy, it was all her. She said I had nothing to do with any of it."

"Yeah, I did. It's how I knew she was lying. If she put the water in the fuel, that was one hell of a long hose she used, because she was already working down here by then. But you knew to go right to the fuel separators to look for water, and tell everybody else about it, trying to stall and keep them from rejoining the show. You knew exactly how to try to sink Smitty, too. Your boat was a few down from his, I saw it when I was up there. You saw Gary leave, but you didn't know he'd be coming back. You were just doing what your friend had done, protecting all the cast from themselves, and me. You told me yourself that you were convinced I was just another Lorne until I pulled Thor out of the fire."

Peter now looked back and forth from his daughter to me, not yet knowing who to believe. I couldn't blame him; nobody wants to believe the worst of their kid. I saw the truth of my words start to sink in though.

Finally, he asked her one question, "Why?"

She sighed heavily, knowing that there was no sense denying it anymore. "Like he said, I was protecting everyone just like Tracy. But mostly I was protecting you. This damn show already cost me mom, or cost us both mom, and I didn't want to lose you, too. I figured Marlin was just as bad and as greedy as Lorne. I didn't know."

Her dad aged ten years in about a minute. In a very sad voice he said, "Honey, your mom and me, it wasn't all about the show. In fact, it started before you were born. It was a lot of things, but being away the past couple of years for tuna season just added to a bunch more we tried to keep hidden from you. I guess it woulda looked like it was all because of the show to you. There was fault and hurt on both our sides."

Peter turned and looked at me, "So, what happens now, you call the cops?"

I looked at Brittney, "Did you help Tracy kill Lorne?"

She looked straight back into my eyes and said with no hesitation, "No. She didn't tell me anything about it until afterward, one night when we'd had too much wine and were sharing things that we wouldn't have otherwise talked about. I swear to you, Marlin, it wasn't until then."

I nodded. "I believe you. No, Peter, no cops. I left everything else except the part about killing Lorne out of my statement. I didn't know why at the time, but I guess I had a hunch. What Brittney did was commit crimes against property, not people. Bad enough by itself, and ordinarily I would've turned anyone in for it. But she tried to save Tracy and she might just have saved Spud; we'll never know for sure. So, here's what we're going to do. For Smitty's part in helping save you, Brittney, you're going to get him a really nice present for his new boat, something a little more expensive than his repair bill cost after you tried sinking him."

Brittney said, "Okay."

I said, "I wasn't finished. I also want you to see a professional psychologist, not just about what happened last night, but about Jason, and about you sabotaging the boats."

"I don't need a shrink, Marlin, I'm not crazy."

"I didn't say you were crazy, and I don't believe that you are. I do however think you have some deep-seated anger and loss issues that you need somebody to help you face. And Kari has a cousin here on ESVA that's top-notch from what I've heard. I want you to make an appointment with her."

Brittney started to object, but I stopped her. "This is a condition for you and your dad staying on the show, and it's not negotiable. While I don't feel that you are a threat to anyone, you've already proven to be willing to damage property. You have to admit, trying to sink a friend's boat isn't a normal reaction to much of anything, and there were much better alternatives to accomplish what you wanted. See, you aren't the only one who is out to protect all these people, it's my job too, and I intend to do my very best, starting with protecting you. Meaning other than with Kari's cousin, none of this goes beyond all of us in this room. Deal?"

She glanced over at her dad who was looking hopeful, then back at me. "Deal, Marlin."

That night Kari and I were lying in bed, talking quietly.

"How did you know, Marlin?"

"Just a hunch, and a lot of hope. Hard to see anger hidden that far down, but once it starts to boil up to the surface, it can really continue to get worse and even become violent."

She said, "Speaking from experience?"

"You know that by rights I should be. But I've always dealt with it by myself out on my boats, thinking it all through. Our boats, that is."

She pulled me close, and we were both asleep in minutes, for the first time in thirty-six hours.

Epilogue

You're probably wondering how tuna season ended up. With Brittney being one-armed for most of it, Peter called in a cousin to help, and he was able to get down here by the first fishing day. They ended up fourth overall in dollar amounts, but first in recovery and rebounds. By the time they headed back north, Brittney had even talked to her mom a few times on the phone. She credited Kari's cousin for it, and was happy I had made her make that first appointment.

Troy Paulson came in third in winnings, but first in impeccably dressed crew and arrogance.

Smitty got edged into second and out of first by a few hundred dollars in the final minutes of the season. I guess you're waiting for me to tell you that it was by Baloney. No such luck. KT and Junior took top honors, as the Pete Jones boats finished in first and second place, making the boat builder another big winner. Last I heard, he now has a waiting list of over two years for a boat.

Like I had dreaded, we ended up with more talent agents circling around than tuna buyers, and all the new cast members will see their per show salaries increase by a minimum two and a half times. Jimbo's calendar is already filled for next season, as is Hard Rock's. KT and Junior have decided to stick with commercial fishing on their own so they can pick their days off. They're also going to do the festival appearance circuit. Both their boats have now been moved to Mallard Cove permanently.

Speaking of Baloney, Spud was back on *My Mahi* in time for the new starting day of the *Tuna Hunters* season. He was fully physically recovered, but still missing Tracy. He hasn't accepted that she killed Lorne, and I doubt he ever will. I'm sure not going to ever bring it up. The day after the end of tuna season, all eight boats filed out in a row to the tuna grounds where we spread Tracy's ashes. That way she'll always be out there with all those she wanted so desperately to protect.

And before you feel too bad about Baloney not winning the season you need to know that I was right about him. According to the experts, his popularity is now on a par with Smitty's, tying the two of them as the top cast member. His new bloodsucker of an agent wanted to play real hardball with me after finding that out. The thing about Bill though is he never forgets a favor, nor who his friends are. We went out for a beer together, leaving the professional bloodsucker at home. We agreed on a figure that, unbeknownst to him, made him the highest-paid boat on the show by two hundred bucks an episode. So, don't tell him that, he doesn't need to know. There'd be no living with him if he did. And yes, of course, he stuck me with the tab for the beer.

As for Kari and me, we'll never look at sushi the same way ever again. We're counting the days until Murph and Linds get back, and until the *Cove Beach Bar* reopens for the season. Then there's that whole wedding thing. She's threatened to have the date, location, and time tattooed on my hand just to remind me not to miss it.

Meanwhile, I got a mysterious call from an old friend, wondering about the marina and if it could handle a big catamaran. He said he might see me soon. I have a real funny feeling about that call...

Marlin, Kari, Murph, Linds and Baloney will return soon in
COASTAL CATS

Additional Mallard Cove Adventure Books:
- ## Coastal Conspiracy
- ## Coastal Cousins
- ## Coastal Paybacks

All are available in Kindle, Paperback, and on Kindle Unlimited.

Author's Notes

Thanks for reading **Coastal Tuna**! If you read this one before reading the first three books in this series, Coastal Conspiracy, Coastal Cousins, and Coastal Paybacks, don't worry. While it's better if they are read in sequence, each can still be read as a "stand alone" book with a minimum of "spoilers". I used the phrase *that's a story for another day* to refer to things that were covered more in depth in those other volumes.

The name *Helena Mary* was borrowed from my friend, **Eric Cottell's** father's classic vessel from many years ago.

Many thanks to my friend from all the way back to our grade school days, **Captain Greg Albritton**, for the spark of inspiration that led to the creation of this story.

Hey, if you liked **Coastal Tuna**, I'd really appreciate it if you wouldn't mind leaving a review on Amazon or Goodreads.com. Just a line or two would be great! If for some reason you didn't like it, please drop me an email instead. You can reach me at contact@donrichbooks.com Actually, please feel free to send me an email even if you liked it, I'd love to hear from you!

I also have a **Reader's Group** where I share pictures and stories that inspire the books. Members also get advance notice of any upcoming releases at discounted rates like those for **Coastal Cats**, the next book of this series which will be coming out in 2020. You can sign up for the Reader's Group on my website, http://www.donrichbooks.com

Printed in Great Britain
by Amazon